HIGH SCHOOL MUSICAL

STORIES FROM EAST HIGH #1

BATTLE OF THE BANDS

By N.B. Grace

Based on the Disney Channel Original Movie
"High School Musical", written by Peter Barsocchini

Disney
PRESS

New York

Printed in the United States of America

First Edition
7 9 10 8

Library of Congress Catalog Card Number on file.
ISBN-13: 978-1-4231-0611-1
ISBN-10: 1-4231-0611-3

For more Disney Press fun, visit www.disneybooks.com
Visit DisneyChannel.com

CHAPTER ONE

The first bell had just rung at East High School when Chad Danforth spotted Troy Bolton across the courtyard.

"Hey, Troy!" Chad yelled, smiling broadly.

But Troy didn't hear him. He was standing with his friend Gabriella Montez. Their heads were bent toward each other as they talked. Troy said something that made Gabriella giggle. Then she said something that made him laugh. Chad rolled his eyes. That was sweet and all, but enough was enough. . . .

"Hey!" Chad called again as he walked toward them, waving his hand in the air. "Troy! What's up?"

Finally, he caught Troy's eye. Gabriella smiled a quick hello at Chad and said, "I'll see you guys at the assembly." Then she waved good-bye. Troy looked after her as she headed inside the building.

"Hey, Troy! How you doin', man?" Chad greeted his friend with a complicated high five, low-five, round-the-back, over-the-top hand-shake.

Troy grinned. Saying hi to Chad was as ath-letic as driving to the hoop for a slam dunk, he thought. "Not bad," he said. "Pretty awesome, in fact."

"Awesome? What happened, did you get an early recruitment call from the NBA?" Chad joked.

"No, I'm just in a really good mood."

Chad raised his eyebrows. "Because . . ."

"Because of Gabriella," Troy said. "You know, I've been spending a lot of time with her."

"Oh, yeah." Chad rolled his eyes. "I know."

Troy got a distracted look on his face. "She's so sweet and smart and talented—"

"Yeah, yeah, yeah." Chad made a get-on-with-it gesture. "I know. We all know."

"What?" His friend looked at him, puzzled by his exasperated tone. "Is something wrong?"

"No. Well, yeah. I mean, not wrong exactly . . . the thing is, I've been meaning to say something. . . ." Chad stopped, flustered.

"Chad, come on! Just tell me! What is it?" Troy tried to laugh, but he was getting worried.

"It's just . . . Gabriella's great and everything, but you're not hanging with your boys anymore. We kinda—" Chad looked nervously over his shoulder to see if anyone was standing close enough to hear him. "—we kinda miss you, dude."

"We see each other every day at practice!" Troy said, surprised.

"Yeah, but Troy, that's not hangin'. You gotta

put in some quality time, especially with me and Jason and Zeke." Chad looked at him earnestly. "The four of us are the core of the team, you know? We gotta stay tight."

"Sure," Troy said. "No problem. I mean, I like doing stuff with you guys, I really do."

Chad grinned, relieved. "Good. We'll set something up. Maybe this weekend? Just the guys."

"Sounds great." Troy smiled and tried not to look worried. He and Gabriella were planning on taking a long bike ride on Saturday and maybe catching a movie on Sunday . . . but hey, there were forty-eight hours in a weekend, right? He could make time for everybody! No problem!

"Come on, let's get to the assembly," he said to Chad. "I heard a rumor that Principal Matsui has a big announcement today. . . ."

Troy and Chad quickly found Gabriella in the auditorium and sat next to her. A few rows behind them, Sharpay and Ryan Evans were sitting with a gaggle of kids from the drama club.

Everyone was chatting about what they did last weekend, what they planned to do next weekend, and how endlessly long the time stretched between weekends.

Finally, Principal Matsui walked onto the stage and tapped the microphone. After a deafening burst of feedback, he called out, "Good morning, East High students! Welcome to another great week of learning and fun!" He paused a moment, waiting for the students to applaud wildly, but—as usual—was met only with quiet murmurs and chuckling.

He sighed and hurried on. "First, a few announcements." He ran down the usual list of SAT preparation classes, pep rallies, and special assemblies. Then he said, "But I have saved the best for last! I'm very excited to announce that the school is going to stage a Battle of the Bands next month in order to raise money for our new tennis courts."

A buzz of excitement filled the auditorium as everyone started whispering to each other.

Troy gave Chad a nudge. "Here's your big chance, buddy. All those years of playing air guitar in your bedroom are finally going to pay off."

"Look who's talking," Chad replied. "Remember when you spent a month practicing air jumps off the couch?"

Gabriella grinned at Troy. "Air jumps? Really?"

"I've got a few moves," Troy said modestly.

"If I may have your attention, please," Principal Matsui said. When the room was quiet enough, he continued. "This is a thrilling opportunity for all you rock stars out there, so I hope we have a big turnout! All you have to do is get a bunch of your friends, form a group, and sign up in the front office by this Friday!"

Sharpay turned to her brother, Ryan, and Alicia and Charlotte, her drama club friends. Well, not exactly *friends*. They were more like girls who were destined to always be understudies, which was, of course, why Sharpay liked them. "We should totally do this!" she said.

"Totally," Ryan agreed with enthusiasm.

Alicia and Charlotte giggled with delight at being chosen by Sharpay.

Principal Matsui finished by saying, "Ms. Dermot will assign rehearsal space on a first-come, first-served basis. Now, it's time for everyone to get to class, but remember—I'm looking forward to hearing a rockin' good show from all of you!"

The students poured into the hall, talking enthusiastically about the Battle of the Bands competition. Sharpay was lost in a daydream, envisioning herself in her favorite spot in the world—onstage, in the spotlight, all eyes fixed on her. . . .

"We'll be awesome!" she said, a note of steely determination in her voice.

"Beyond awesome!" Ryan interjected. "Awesome to the tenth power!"

His sister shot him a confused look. Sometimes she had no idea what Ryan was talking about. "First of all," she said, firmly regaining control of the conversation, "what could be more perfect than me as the lead singer—"

"Absolutely," Ryan said.

"And you two—" She indicated Alicia and Charlotte. "—as backup singers—"

"Of course." The girls nodded obediently.

"—of an absolutely fabulous girl group!" Sharpay finished.

"Um . . . girl group?" Ryan echoed.

"Yes!" she cried. "It'll be so retro!"

"But, Sharpay, if it's a *girl* group . . ." Ryan stopped, puzzled, then tried again. "I mean, what about me?"

Sharpay ignored him. "We'll wear miniskirts and knee-high boots and have our hair done in that sixties style," she said, thinking out loud. "And of course, we need a really cool song—"

"Sharpay?" Ryan tried again. "When you say 'girl group,' do you mean that it will actually have, um, only girls in it?"

"What?" His sister stared at him blankly. "Well, of course, Ryan! What a silly question!"

She turned back to her friends. As they began

chatting eagerly about song possibilities, Sharpay didn't notice Ryan's crestfallen look, his slumped shoulders, or the way his feet dragged as he walked slowly away.

"Now, we'll have to pick a song that really showcases the lead singer," she was saying. "Not to mention a song that offers the possibility of some showstopping choreography . . ."

Gabriella, Troy, and Chad continued their conversation as they left the auditorium. "So what are your best rock-star moves?" Gabriella asked Troy, a teasing note in her voice.

He shrugged, grinning. "Oh, you know. The windmill—" He pantomimed swinging his arm around and strumming chords. "—the head bob—" He nodded his head in time to imaginary music. "Just stupid stuff like that."

"That's not all," Chad said to Gabriella. "He actually knows how to play guitar."

"Well . . . only three chords," Troy said. "But that's all you need to play ninety-five percent of all rock songs ever written, so . . ." He stopped dead in his tracks and looked at Chad. "Hey! I just had a great idea!"

Chad raised his eyebrows.

"We could form a band!" Troy said eagerly. "I could teach you guys how to play guitar—well, three chords, anyway."

"Awesome!" Chad's eyes lit up at the idea of taking the stage in full rock-star mode.

Gabriella's eyes sparkled. "That's such a good idea—"

"And you know how you were saying that I needed to hang with the guys more?" Troy went on to Chad. "This is a perfect way to do that! We can hang out and jam together, just us guys!"

Gabriella's smile dimmed. "Oh. You're going to be in a band with your basketball friends."

"Yeah!" Troy turned to her, grinning with excitement. He didn't notice how flat her voice was, or the way she tried to smile but couldn't quite manage it, or the way she bit her lip with disappointment. "Man, this is going to be awesome!"

"You got that right!" Chad was grinning, too. "Now, the first thing we need is a cool name. That's key. An awesome name can *make* a band. How about The Three-Pointers?"

"The Three-Pointers?" Troy repeated dubiously. "Um, I don't know . . . doesn't that make it sound like there are only three of us? And we're a pack of hunting dogs?"

"C'mon, man, it's perfect! No? Okay, how about B-Ball Boyz?"

As they turned the corner, still debating band names, Gabriella headed for her first class. It's ridiculous to feel disappointed that Troy wants to put together a band without me, she thought. After all, she was going to see him at lunch, and they were going to grab some pizza after school, and they had already made plans for next weekend. . . . She was going to have plenty of chances to hang out with him.

So why, she wondered, do I suddenly feel so left out?

11

CHAPTER TWO

"Okay, guys, let's start with some drills," Troy called out. He was in the gym with the rest of the basketball team. They bounded onto the court, slapping high fives and grinning.

"Time to catch some Wildcat fever!" Chad yelled as he grabbed a ball and threw it to Jason Cross.

Jason spun and threw the ball to Zeke Baylor, who caught it easily and tossed it to Troy.

"Great job," Troy said. "Now, pick up the pace. . . ."

As they practiced their passing skills, they moved faster and faster. The ball spun through the air. No one dropped it, no one fumbled, no one missed a step—they were definitely in a groove today!

By the end of the drill, they were sweaty and happy. There was nothing like the feeling of working together as a team, Troy thought. They had been playing together for so long that they could anticipate each other's moves and get the ball to the right person at the right time without even thinking about it. It was like they were all moving to the same rhythm, feeling the same beat, listening to the same drummer—

"I could be the drummer," Jason was saying.

Troy snapped to attention. "What did you say?"

Jason threw the ball to him and they started doing layup drills. "I said, I could be the drummer for the band. I could use my dad's drum kit. It's been sitting in the attic for about ten years, but I just need to dust it off and I'll be good to go."

"I can borrow my brother's bass," Zeke said eagerly.

Troy shot Chad a look.

"I guess I kinda told the guys our idea already," Chad said. "Sorry."

"Oh. Well, cool." Troy shrugged, trying to look casual. He thought he'd be the one to tell the guys; after all, it was his idea, wasn't it? But he knew Chad was excited about the band. It wasn't that big of a deal that he'd told them.

"Hey, what are we going to call the band?" Chad said.

"I thought I'd come up with something tonight," Troy said. Of course, he had a lot of homework to do, but the band name was way too important to leave to the last minute—

" 'Cause I'm really good at things like coming up with band names!" Chad said, interrupting his thoughts.

Troy said, "Well, actually, I've already started brainstorming some ideas—"

"How about Blink 68–67?" Chad suggested

eagerly. "It's perfect, because we won the championship game, 68–67, and if you *blinked*, you would have missed it!"

"Um . . ." Troy said. "That's a little derivative, don't you think?"

Chad shrugged cheerfully. "Okay. If that name doesn't work, I've got a million more!"

"We better start thinking about our set list," Jason chimed in. "How many songs do we get to play in the competition?"

"I'm not sure," Troy answered. "I'll check when I sign us up and then we can talk about it—"

" 'Cause, dude, I totally think we should do 'We Are the Champions'! That's the most rockin' song ever! Not to mention *extremely* appropriate for members of the Wildcats basketball team!"

Troy shook his head. "I think we should pick something that people can dance to," he said. "Don't worry, I'll think of something. Now, c'mon, guys, we gotta focus on *basketball* right now."

"Yes, sir, captain, sir." Chad saluted him with a grin and passed him the ball.

Troy dribbled downcourt and made a basket. *Swish!* Nothing but net!

He grinned. Now he felt like his old self: on top of his game and in control.

Basketball practice was in full swing in the gym while Gabriella was walking down the hall to room 154, feeling just a little nervous. A few weeks ago, the school counselor had announced that she was organizing a peer-tutoring program so that students who had a firm grasp of certain subjects could help others who were struggling.

At the time, Gabriella had thought that this would be the perfect extracurricular activity for her. After all, she made straight A's every semester, and she liked helping other students when they were struggling to understand something in class. . . . So, in what she now considered a moment of madness, she had signed up.

Her forehead was creased with worry as she

approached the classroom where she would meet, for the first time, the person she had been assigned to tutor in algebra. What if the person didn't like her? What if she couldn't explain the math concepts clearly? What if she tried her very best and still failed?

She bit her lip as she swung the door open . . . and saw Ryan Evans sitting at a desk, looking just as anxious as she felt.

"You're my tutor?" he asked, shocked. Sharpay, he thought, was going to freak when she found out that the girl who beat her out for the lead role in the school musical was teaching him. True, she and Gabriella had come to an uneasy truce by the time *Twinkle Towne* ended its run, but Sharpay still had a chip on her shoulder about having *any* kind of competition in the world of showbiz—let alone *good* competition.

"I guess so." Gabriella decided to double-check. "Algebra two, right?"

"Yeah, that's me," he said dolefully. "I'm a complete dunce when it comes to math."

"Oh, I'm sure that's not true." She smiled as she sat down next to him. "I mean, you're such a good singer!"

He eyed her suspiciously. "Yeah . . ." he said slowly, "but what does that have to do with math?"

"Well, counting out beats is math, right?" she said brightly, trying to sound self-assured. She had actually just wanted to boost Ryan's confidence, but now that she thought about it, his singing ability probably wasn't going to translate too well into solving equations.

Fortunately, Ryan really *didn't* know much about algebra. He looked happy and relieved at her reasoning. "That's true!" he cried. "I never thought about it that way before!"

Gabriella nodded earnestly. "And if you can remember all the steps to a complicated dance routine, you can certainly remember algebraic formulas!"

"That's an *excellent* point." Ryan was totally with her now. I don't know why Sharpay thinks

Gabriella is so irritating, he thought. She seems really nice.

"And if you can figure out how to do choreography with ten dancers when three of them are left-handed, two of them can't kick above their waists, and four of them are klutzes, then handling variables should be a breeze!" Gabriella concluded brightly.

"Oh, um . . . really?" Ryan looked unsure, and she realized that she had lost him by introducing variables into the metaphor.

"Absolutely!" she said, with as much conviction as she could muster. "But we're getting ahead of ourselves. Why don't we take a look at the work you're doing now. . . ."

An hour later, Gabriella had led Ryan through a torturous word problem involving two cars traveling at different rates of speed from opposite directions. He finally understood how to solve the problem when she changed the story line a bit, explaining that car A was packed with costumes for a play at a local dinner theater, while car B's passengers were heading to a summer-stock audition.

"I think the answer is, um, two hours?" Ryan said.

"Awesome!" Gabriella exclaimed. She breathed a private sigh of relief. "You're absolutely right!"

"I . . . I am?" He looked stunned. "Are you sure? I'm hardly ever right. At least, that's what Sharpay says—"

"Yes, I'm sure! See, algebra's not so hard once you break it down."

"Not the way you explain it," he said. "It seems to make so much more sense than when Mrs. Jefferson tries to teach it."

"Well, that's what peer tutoring is all about, right? Getting some help, one-on-one . . ." Gabriella glanced at her watch. "Oh, no, it's already five o'clock! I'm sorry, I've got to go. Troy and I are going to get some pizza."

"Oh, sure." Ryan looked disappointed. "Hey,

are you and Troy going to enter the Battle of the Bands? Sharpay said you probably would. . . ."

A shadow passed over her face, but she said brightly, "No, I think Troy's going to do something with some of his friends from the team."

Hmm, Ryan thought. Sharpay will be very interested to hear that!

But Gabriella was asking him a question. . . .

"So what do you and Sharpay have planned?"

"Nothing," he said, disgruntled. "Well, *Sharpay* has something planned. She wants to form a girl group." He gave a snort of disgust. "Like *that's* going to get a lot of votes!"

"Oh, well," she said philosophically, "we can't all be stars all the time, I guess."

Ryan's mouth hung open in shock. What was she saying? *We. Can't. All. Be. Stars . . . ?*

But before he could respond, she had turned on her PDA. "Hmm . . . how about meeting next Wednesday?"

"Great." Ryan smiled. He had been feeling so lonely today and had been dreading this tutoring

session so much, but it had actually worked out well. Very well, in fact. "I'll be *counting* the days."
He waited a second. "Get it? Counting the days?"

"Oh!" Gabriella did her best to laugh. "Very funny. Well, I gotta run! See you later!"

CHAPTER THREE

The next morning, Troy went to the school office to sign up his band for the competition. As he entered, he saw Sharpay carefully writing her name on the sign-up sheet in her usual huge, loopy handwriting. He peered over her shoulder.

"Are you sure everyone can read your name, Sharpay?" he asked, deadpan. "You might want to make it a little bigger."

She tossed her head in exasperation, her blond hair flying. "You're always making jokes,

Troy, but this time, I will have the last laugh! People are going to be stunned by my group's performance! You and your . . . *Neanderthal basketball players* don't stand a chance."

Troy had only been teasing, but he didn't like the way she sneered when she said "Neanderthal basketball players." It sounded like she thought they weren't in her league, musically speaking— or that there was something wrong with basketball players. Or Neanderthals, for that matter.

"Hey, listen, we are going to *rock the house*!" he said, trying to inject a note of confident bravado into his voice.

"Oh, yes, I'm sure you will," Sharpay said with a poisonously sweet smile. "But this isn't about making a lot of noise. It's about talent— and I . . . that is, *my group*, has that in spades!"

"Oh, yeah?" Troy eyed her suspiciously. "Who else is in your group, anyway?"

She hesitated, then said, "That's a secret for right now. But believe me, we are going to win! In fact—" She turned to Ms. Dermot, the school secretary, who had been watching Troy and Sharpay's minismackdown with amazement. "—you might want to keep that sign-up sheet with my autograph. It's going to be worth a lot some day!"

She flounced out of the office. As Troy watched her go, he thought, Hmm, I wonder what she has planned. . . .

Sharpay's plan was actually quite simple. Find three other girls who could sing on key, master simple choreography, and be willing to stand behind her onstage, singing nothing but "Oh, yeah" and "Mmm-hmm" without complaining. She already had Alicia and Charlotte, of course— face it, she had them at hello—but she needed one more girl to complete the group.

As she walked down the hall, she passed the choir room. Inside, the school choir was already practicing for the holiday concert. As they swung into a spirited version of "Here Comes Santa Claus," Sharpay smirked. Choir was all right if you wanted to sing with fifty other people, she thought. But for gifted performers like herself, who should always be singing solo, it was just too, too . . . *anonymous*.

Even as she had that thought, the bell rang and the members of the choir came pouring out the door, chattering among themselves as they headed for their next class. Sharpay pushed her way into the room, where she spotted the choir teacher.

"Excuse me!" she called out officiously. "Excuse me! I need to talk to you!"

Mrs. Jones raised her eyebrows at this pushy girl, but she nodded. "Can I help you?"

"My name is Sharpay Evans." Sharpay waited for the woman to realize who she was.

Mrs. Jones merely gave her an inquiring look. "Yes?"

"Well, I wanted . . . that is, I just wondered—" Sharpay floundered as she spoke. She couldn't believe Mrs. Jones didn't know who she was! She took a deep breath and started over. "I'm putting together a girl group for the Battle of the Bands," she explained. "I have two backup singers, but I need another one." Her gaze swept dismissively over the choir room. "I'm sure at least *one* of your singers will meet my standards."

"Ah, I see." The teacher nodded. "I'm sure I can recommend someone of the right . . . level for what you want," she added, hiding a smile. "In fact, I think Taylor McKessie would be *perfect*."

"Taylor? Really?" Sharpay squinted into the distance, trying to bring Taylor to mind. Ah, yes. Beautiful. Brainiac. Boring. "She can sing?"

"I think you'll find her talent quite acceptable," the teacher said solemnly. She gave Sharpay a little wink.

"Oh, great!" Sharpay was relieved. There was no chance she'd be upstaged by someone whose talent was merely acceptable. "She sounds just right."

The teacher nodded. "I'm sure she will be." As Sharpay headed out the door, she called out, "Good luck!"

Sharpay gave her a disdainful smile. As if luck

had anything to do with winning, she thought smugly.

Taylor was hunched over a lab table in chemistry, rereading her scrawled notes as she waited for class to begin. She really didn't need to refresh her memory—she was already reading ahead in the textbook just for fun—but she wanted to get her mind off that disastrous choir practice.

The choir teacher had warned her about letting her voice overpower the other singers. "You have a powerful instrument," Mrs. Jones had told her privately, soon after she joined the choir.

"And that's bad?" Taylor was confused.

"No, no, it's good—if the rest of the singers could match it," Mrs. Jones had explained. "But their singing just isn't as strong, so your voice throws the whole choir out of balance."

"Oh." Taylor always thought she had a good voice. Now she was beginning to wonder if she actually sounded like a braying donkey when she sang.

Mrs. Jones had smiled at her kindly. "I'm sure I'll be able to give you a solo at some point. I just have to wait a while, since you're so new to the choir. Then you'll be able to let loose! But in the meantime, if you wouldn't mind exercising a little restraint?"

Taylor had nodded glumly. And she had tried, she really had. But in today's rehearsal, Mrs. Jones still had to warn her three times to tone it down a bit. She had seen a few of the choir members exchange meaningful looks—a raised eyebrow here, a roll of the eyes there—and she had bitten her lip with embarrassment. She suspected that they all thought she was some kind of diva, which was so absolutely not true! She would never demand attention, fight for the spotlight, or upstage someone else! She would never, for example, be like Sharpay—

"Hey, Taylor!"

Taylor jumped. Sharpay was standing in front of her lab table, smiling.

"What are you doing here?" Taylor asked. No

one would ever expect to see Sharpay in the advanced chemistry class! Taylor almost felt that she had conjured the drama princess through her own thoughts. . . .

"I'm here to offer you an incredible opportunity!" Sharpay cried.

"And what is that?" Taylor asked cautiously. The girl sounded like a telemarketer, pitching a dubious and shady scheme. "A once-in-a-lifetime chance to invest in your next musical?"

"No, silly! Although—" Sharpay looked thoughtful. "—that's not a bad idea. . . ."

Taylor sighed. What was the use of sarcasm if it flew right over the victim's head? "Sharpay, class is about to start. If you don't want to be trapped here figuring out the pH balance of different liquids, tell me what you want."

"Okay, listen. I'm putting together a girl group for the Battle of the Bands. I'll be lead singer, of course, but I need some really talented backup singers. I asked Mrs. Jones for recommendations, and she said you would be perfect!

So . . ." Sharpay paused for a breath. "What do you think?"

"Mrs. Jones recommended me? Really?"

Sharpay nodded. Taylor sat still for a minute, thinking hard. Mrs. Jones had seen how difficult it was for her to hold back in her singing today. Maybe she thought Taylor needed practice staying in the background? Maybe she thought she needed to learn to blend in a little more? Maybe she was trying to tell Taylor that she shouldn't be thinking of solos just yet, that she had to earn the chance to sing the lead? Taylor felt chastened. Mrs. Jones, she thought, is trying to teach me to be humble. That's the only reason she could have suggested that I sing backup behind someone like Sharpay!

Well, Taylor took pride in her willingness to learn the lessons she needed in order to succeed. She was not an egotistical airhead like some people she could mention! It would be tough to stand in the background and support Sharpay, but she knew it be would good for her in the long run. Taylor nodded to herself, her decision made.

"All right," she said to Sharpay, gritting her teeth. "I'll do it."

Sharpay's eyes widened in an expression of delight that could have been seen from the back balcony, had she actually been onstage. "Wonderful!" she exclaimed.

At that moment, Gabriella rushed in and pulled a lab stool up to the table. "Whew, can't believe I made it before the bell!" she said. She looked at Sharpay and Taylor as she pulled a notebook out of her backpack. "So, what's so wonderful?"

"Taylor's joining my group for the Battle of the Bands," Sharpay said smugly.

"Really?" Gabriella gave her friend a questioning look. "That's . . . um . . . great."

"I'll explain later," Taylor whispered. She turned to Sharpay. "Hey, maybe Gabriella could join, too! She has an awesome voice—"

"Sorry, no." Sharpay's smile was strained.

"It's a four-girl group. You're the fourth girl."

"Would it be so hard to make it a five-girl group?" Taylor asked. This would be so much more fun if Gabriella were involved. . . .

There was a brief, awkward silence.

"That's okay," Gabriella said quickly. "I'm really busy right now, anyway. You know, studying for the SAT, peer tutoring, all that stuff."

Sharpay smiled more warmly. "Well, this works out perfectly then, doesn't it?" She gave Taylor a little wave as she said, "First rehearsal tomorrow after school, in the choir room. I'll give you your music then. See you!"

As Sharpay flounced out of the room, Gabriella said, "*You* are singing backup for Sharpay?"

Taylor sighed. "Long story. I'll tell you after class."

Chemistry class was over right before lunch. Gabriella and Taylor took their sandwiches to a table outside and sat down.

"So?" Gabriella said. "What's going on? I can't believe you joined Sharpay's group!"

"Yeah, I know." Taylor started to carefully disassemble the healthy turkey sandwich—filled with lettuce, tomatoes, and bean sprouts—that her mother insisted on making for her at least three times a week. "That girl is whacked out! But Mrs. Jones is an awesome choir director, so when I found out that she recommended me, I figured she must have a good reason." She shrugged and looked down, concentrating on the task of rebuilding her sandwich with just the bread and turkey slices.

"Mmm." Gabriella frowned at the leftover pile of veggies. "Well, I'm sure it will be a lot of fun."

Taylor looked at her questioningly. "You're not upset, are you? About not being in the group?"

"Oh, of course not!" Gabriella said airily. "I mean, Sharpay and I get along okay now, but it would still be pretty awkward to be singing with her. Plus, if I sang in her group, I'd be competing against Troy and, well . . ." She blushed, and Taylor gave her a knowing look.

"Uh-huh," Taylor said. "So what's the latest with you and that boy?"

"Well, since you *ask* . . ." Gabriella smiled and devoted the next hour to giving her friend a minute-by-minute description of the bike ride they took last weekend and discussing what kind of dress she should buy for the prom.

CHAPTER FOUR

"**O**kay, guys, let's get started!" Troy had to raise his voice to be heard over the cacophony that was being produced on the auditorium stage of East High School. Apparently, he didn't raise it enough.

Jason was banging away on his dad's drum kit. He seemed to be particularly fond of hitting the cymbals. Zeke was plunking with great enthusiasm—but no real skill—at his bass guitar. Chad was re-creating the most awesome riffs from his favorite heavy metal bands. He actually sounded pretty good, Troy thought. But loud. Very, very loud.

"Guys!" Troy yelled. "Hey!"

Still no reaction. Finally, he put two fingers in his mouth and blew an ear-piercing whistle. Everyone stopped playing to look at him in surprise.

"Hey, dude, we're not in basketball practice right now," Chad said.

"Oh, yeah." Troy shuffled his feet, embarrassed. "Sorry about that. I just thought we should discuss a few things before we start playing—"

"Jammin'," Zeke said firmly. "We're not just playing, man. We're *jammin'*."

"Oh, yeah, right." Troy picked up his guitar. "But before we get started, um, jamming, maybe we should talk about a few things? Like what song we're going to play and—"

"—and the name of the band!" Chad shouted. "I got another one! New Kidz on the Court!"

"Too girly," Zeke objected.

"Yeah, sounds like a boy band," Jason agreed.

"Okay," Chad said, undaunted, "how about the Mighty Mighty B'Ball Tones? No? Well, what about No Foul—"

As the other boys continued to argue, Troy sighed and strummed a few lonely chords on his guitar.

"Okay, everyone, let's get started!" Sharpay clapped her hands. "Quiet, please!"

Alicia and Charlotte instantly fell silent. Taylor raised one eyebrow at Sharpay's high-handed attitude, but then she shrugged. Sharpay was the leader of this group, after all. She could run it the way she wanted.

"Thank you. Now, here is your music." Sharpay began passing out pages of sheet music. "I thought we would sing 'Stop! In the Name of Love.' It's a real old-school song from like, I don't know, the sixties—"

"1965," Taylor said helpfully. "Originally sung by The Supremes. It went to number one on the charts and it was nominated for a Grammy. . . ."

"Oh, right." Sharpay stared at her for a long, displeased moment.

"Good choice," Taylor offered peaceably, and Sharpay relaxed.

"Thanks. So I'll give you a few minutes to go over your score, and then we can give it a try!"

The other girls obediently began flipping through their music, mouthing the words as they did so. Taylor pretended to look at hers, though she didn't need to. Her mother loved sixties music, so she had grown up singing these songs. She hummed a bit, smiling. This could actually be fun. . . .

"Now, I've figured out exactly what kind of costumes we're going to wear," Sharpay said. She quickly passed out photocopies of sketches she had created the night before. The costumes were black miniskirts, white halter tops, white knee-high boots, and huge white earrings. Every girl's hair was teased into a bouffant hairdo.

Taylor nodded in appreciation. "Groovy."

Sharpay gave her a warm smile. "Thanks, Taylor! I want us to look and sing just like The Supremes—only better!"

Taylor raised one eyebrow. Better than The Supremes? Talk about setting the bar high.

"Um, Sharpay?" Alicia said timidly. "Who are The Supremes?"

Taylor was so shocked she didn't wait for Sharpay to answer. "Only the best girl group of all time!" she cried. "They were one of the biggest acts in Motown! They had twelve number one hits in the sixties, like 'Baby Love' and 'You Can't Hurry Love'! Not to mention—"

But Sharpay's eyes were glinting at her again. Too late, Taylor closed her mouth.

"Thank you for that history lesson, Taylor," she said icily. "But I think it's time we started re-hearsing *our* song, don't you?" Sharpay turned on a boom box and began singing along to the music.

Give the girl credit, Taylor thought. She's giving a full-on performance, even though there are only three people listening. If nothing else, she's committed to her art.

Sharpay made a gesture for the other girls to come in with the background vocals. They started singing, a little raggedly in Charlotte's case, and Sharpay smiled. Her voice got louder, and the backup singers swayed and doo-wopped away.

Taylor was in the groove, feeling fine, when she suddenly noticed that everyone else had stopped singing. They were all staring at her.

"Umm . . . what?" She had a sinking feeling in her stomach.

"Wow!" Alicia said, wide-eyed. "You're really good!"

"Good? You're awesome!" Charlotte added.

"Yes." Sharpay could barely squeeze the word out through her clenched teeth. "I had no idea, Taylor, what a big voice you have."

"Sorry. I'll try to tone it down," Taylor said sheepishly.

"Do that." Sharpay's words were clipped and icy. "Now, let's start again. From the top . . ."

CHAPTER FIVE

When Gabriella walked into room 154 for the next tutoring session, she found Ryan already there. He was dancing in front of the blackboard to the accompaniment of a song he was singing. The drama teacher, Ms. Darbus, was sitting in the front row of desks watching him appraisingly.

Gabriella stopped, confused. She was supposed to be tutoring him, wasn't she? She checked her watch. Yes, it was time for their appointment. But why was Ms. Darbus here? And why was Ryan singing, "Stop! In the Name of Love"? And why was he *dancing*?

Ryan caught sight of Gabriella, but he didn't stop out of embarrassment, as most kids would have. Instead, he finished with a dramatic flourish, spinning around a few times and ending with both hands pointing at Gabriella. She applauded weakly, because he clearly expected her to. Ms. Darbus stood up, applauding wildly and yelling, "Bravo!"

"Thanks, Ms. Darbus!" he said, a little out of breath. He turned to Gabriella and asked, "What do you think? Pretty spectacular, huh?"

"Yeah, it's, um . . . spectacular, all right," she echoed. That seemed to be the safest response.

It worked. He grinned and said, "I'm working up some choreography for Sharpay's group."

"Oh, that's great!" Gabriella said sincerely. She knew he had been feeling left out.

He shrugged. "Not as great as singing on-stage. But Sharpay always talks about how even

43

the little people behind the scenes have their role to play in making someone a star." He sighed deeply. "I just never thought that *I* would be one of the little people."

"Yeah, I know," she said wistfully.

He cocked his head to one side, puzzled. "What do you mean? After your performance in *Twinkle Towne*, you became a star! *You* would never be forced to sit backstage, watching while other selfish people stole the spotlight for themselves using some egotistical ploy—"

"I wouldn't be too sure of that," she interrupted, sensing that he was working his way into a full-blown tantrum. "I mean, not that I care, really, but I'm not singing in the Battle of the Bands either."

Ms. Darbus had been listening to their conversation in silence. Now she stepped forward, her eyes flashing.

"That is utterly absurd!" she cried.

"Um . . . excuse me?" Gabriella said.

"A singer of your talent is not going to be

represented in the Battle of the Bands? Ridiculous!"

Gabriella smiled at the compliment, then shook her head. "Well, it *is* called the Battle of the Bands," she pointed out. "I wasn't asked to join a band, so—"

"What about Troy's band?" Ryan said. "Can't you join that?"

She shrugged. "He's playing with his basketball buddies. It's a chance for them to, you know . . . bond. I wouldn't want to get in the way of that."

"Oh." Ryan looked at her with the heartfelt sympathy of another supremely talented person who has been unfairly overlooked. "That's too bad."

"No, no, it's fine!" Gabriella did her best to give a carefree laugh. "There are always other chances to sing, right?"

"Right." Ryan didn't sound convinced.

"Wrong!" Ms. Darbus snapped. "Read the rules of the competition more closely. The Battle of the Bands is open to any group or *singer* who wants to enter. And you, Ms. Montez, are a singer. Now, I want you to march right down to the office and sign up for a solo. Now."

"But, but, but—" Gabriella stammered.

Ryan's eyes were alight with excitement. "You'll be the only solo singer! You'll stand out! You might even win!"

"But I don't want to stand out—"

"Nonsense!" Ms. Darbus waved away her protest. "A girl of your talent shouldn't be in the audience, applauding other people! You should be onstage, basking in others' applause!"

"Thank you, but I—"

Ms. Darbus clapped her hands in glee. "Good! Then it's decided! You don't even have to go to the office. I'm going to a meeting with Principal Matsui, so I'll sign you up while I'm there. And I'll ask Kelsi Neilsen to be your accompanist. I know she'll be glad to help out. Now, the only question left is what you should sing—but I'm sure I'll come up with something by tomorrow."

"I'm not sure—" Gabriella said weakly, trying in vain to backtrack from the commitment she had somehow just made to compete in the Battle of the Bands.

"Of course you're not! That's why Ryan and I are here to urge you on." Ms. Darbus said.

Ryan nodded enthusiastically. "You'll be great, Gabriella," he said.

She smiled, softened by his obvious sincerity. "Well . . . all right."

"Excellent! Come by my classroom at noon tomorrow and we'll begin working!" the drama teacher said. "Until then!"

She swept out of the room. Ryan and Gabriella stared at each other, a little surprised and shocked by what had just happened. Ryan grinned at her. "You're going to be so great!" he said, excited.

"Well, we'll see," she answered, but her eyes were sparkling. "Now, we'd better get to work," she added firmly. "Let's start with the problems on page thirty-two. . . ."

"Hey, Troy!" Gabriella smiled as she called out from backstage.

Troy and his band had just finished a disastrous attempt at a hard-rocking remake of "Twist and Shout." He smiled back when he saw her, but he was clearly distracted. "Oh, hi, Gabriella."

He turned to the band. "Let's take five, okay, guys?"

They nodded and started chatting as Troy walked over to her. "I'm sorry, I can't talk long. I think we're going to have to rehearse for a while longer."

"Oh." Her smile dimmed. "I thought we were going to catch a movie—"

"I know, I know." He sighed. "I'd like to, but we really need the practice."

"Of course," she said, putting a hand on his arm. "I totally understand. Especially since—"

"Yes?" he asked.

Gabriella bit her lip. She had wanted to tell him about singing a solo in the competition, but this just wasn't the moment. He was barely able to pay any attention to her at all! "Oh, nothing," she said, just as Zeke ran up.

"I'm getting a soda," Zeke said. "You guys want anything?"

"No, thanks," Troy said. "Hey, don't be too long, okay? We have a lot of work to do."

Zeke pointed at Troy and winked. "No worries, bro. I'll be back in a flash!"

As he ran out the door, Troy sighed and turned back to Gabriella. "Sorry about that," he said. "We haven't started on time yet and . . . anyway. What were you saying?"

She brightened up a bit. "Oh, well, I was going to tell you that—"

"Hey, Gabriella, did you hear that last song?" Chad called out. "How did we sound? Awesome, right?"

"I just caught the end of it. You guys sound really—" She hesitated. *Good* wasn't exactly the right word. "—like you've been working hard," she finished tactfully.

"Yeah!" Jason nodded eagerly. "We'll have this song nailed in a couple of days."

"I don't know about that. . . ." Troy looked skeptical.

"Okay, maybe a week," Jason admitted. "At the most."

Troy ran his hand through his hair in frustration. "It's not just playing the song," he said. "We gotta look like a rock band! But all we do is stand on the stage, like our feet are glued in one place."

Zeke returned with his can of soda, but found the other boys looking downcast. "You're right," Chad said. "It's a lot easier to jump around when you're playing air guitar. But, man, with a real guitar—you gotta play all the right notes in the right order and everything!"

Jason and Zeke nodded in agreement.

"Well, we have to figure this out," Troy said, feeling a little lost. "Somehow." If this were basketball, he thought, we could run drills. But what kind of drills do you run in order to look like real rockers?

Gabriella cleared her throat. "Um . . . could I make a suggestion?"

They all turned to look at her.

"Yeah, sure," Zeke said. "We need help! Any kind of help!"

"Well, Ryan Evans told me that he's doing choreography for Sharpay's group—"

The boys all looked uneasily at each other.

"I don't know if we want, um . . . *choreography*," Chad said.

"Yeah, we need something more like . . . like *moves*, you know?" Zeke chimed in.

"But that's what choreography *is*!" Gabriella cried. "And Ryan really is very good."

"Would he help us?" Troy asked. "I mean, Sharpay pretty much calls the shots, right? She won't be happy about anything that will give us an advantage."

Gabriella shrugged. "I don't know. But it wouldn't hurt to ask. . . ."

The boys hesitated, then nodded. As they started discussing who should approach Ryan,

Gabriella decided that she could always tell Troy about her decision to enter the Battle of the Bands later—when he had more time to focus on her, instead of the band.

Troy tucked the idea of talking to Ryan in the back of his mind and didn't think about it for a few days. Then he and the guys showed up in the auditorium to rehearse, only to find that Sharpay and her singers were already on the stage!

"Okay, everyone," she said bossily to Taylor, Alicia, and Charlotte. "Line up behind me. No— farther back. I'm going to need at least three feet between us, right, Ryan?"

Ryan was standing to one side, arms folded, watching them critically. "At least," he agreed. "You're going to have to spin around, then do a couple of high kicks—three feet is the minimum amount of clearance you'll need. Five feet might be better."

Alicia and Charlotte quickly scooted back a few feet, but Taylor stood her ground. "There's going to be a curtain across the back of the stage, right?" she said. "We'll run into it if we back up five feet—"

Sharpay waved a dismissive hand. "We'll figure that out in dress rehearsal," she said breezily. "Now, back, back . . ."

Troy stepped forward. "Excuse me," he said.

"Oh, hi, Troy!" Sharpay gave him a big smile. "I'm so excited about the Battle of the Bands, aren't you?"

"Um, sure. But there's something we need to discuss—" Troy began.

"I mean, I know we're competitors and everything, but that doesn't mean we can't be *friendly* competitors, does it?" she purred.

"Absolutely not." Troy nodded agreeably. "Winning some trophy isn't really the point, anyway, right? This is about having fun and raising money for the new tennis courts."

Winning wasn't the point? Sharpay's smile slipped for a moment in confusion, but she recovered quickly. "You are so right, Troy," she went on. "You and I think *so* much alike! But that makes sense, doesn't it, since we have so much in common? We both have a musical vision, of course. And *I'm* the musical leader of *my* incredible singing group, and *you're* in charge of your—" She glanced at Chad, Zeke, and Jason, and smiled condescendingly. "—little band."

Troy just grinned. No chance of getting a big ego around Sharpay, he thought. She would always be able to cut you down to size.

But the other boys took her remark more personally.

"Dude, who is she calling a little band?" Zeke muttered to Jason. "She makes us sound like The Wiggles."

Jason shook his head in disbelief. "We're not little," he muttered back. "We're hard-core."

Troy said to Sharpay, "Yeah, but see, the thing is . . . we booked the stage from four to six." He glanced at his watch and added, "It's 4:05. So . . ."

"So . . . you must have gotten the time wrong," she said, tossing her hair. "*We* booked it from three to seven. And we're not giving it up."

Okay, Troy thought. So much for friendly competition.

"No way we got our time wrong," Chad said. "I stopped by the office myself to sign us up!"

"Oh?" she said disdainfully. "So you can actually write?"

Ryan, Alicia, and Charlotte simpered at her wisecrack.

"Anyway," she went on, "we're all set up now, so it makes more sense for you to come back another time. Let's see, I have the room reserved until seven o'clock, but I don't want to be unreasonable. . . . How about if you come back at, oh, say, 6:55?"

"Oh?" Chad said, mimicking her tone. "So you can actually tell time?"

Zeke and Jason cracked up. Troy tried to keep a straight face, but he couldn't help smiling just a little.

"Look," he said reasonably, "maybe we can compromise—"

Sharpay's chin lifted an inch. Ryan shuddered. He knew what it meant when she lifted her chin. . . .

"No compromise," she said icily. "Rules are rules. I signed up for four hours, and I am going to rehearse for four hours!"

"But, Sharpay, isn't that a little . . . extreme?" Troy ran his hands through his hair in frustration. "We only have three weeks until the Battle of the Bands!" He gave her a winning smile. "Couldn't you cut your rehearsal short, just this one time?"

Sharpay tilted her head to look at him. She relaxed a tiny bit. A small smile even tugged at her lips. "Well," she said, "since you're asking so nicely—"

"And the Troy Bolton charm works again!" Chad muttered to Jason, who laughed and gave him a high five.

Unfortunately, Sharpay heard the comment as well. Her face darkened. Did they think she could be manipulated by a boyish grin and a winsome manner? She had been in show business a long, long time—long enough to know all about back-stage plotting and duplicitous, two-faced, sneaky charmers who just wanted to get their own way!

So she straightened her spine and gave Troy Bolton and his buddies her best diva glare. "Forget it!" Sharpay snapped. "We are going to use our full rehearsal time. And when it's time for the competition, we'll see who has true talent and who needs to go back to playing air guitar! In fact, I want to put you and your band on notice. We are going to *take you down*."

Troy stood up a little straighter at that. He had wanted to be easygoing about all this, but her challenge had just kicked his competitive spirit into high gear. Forget about friendly competition, he thought. Forget about just having fun and not caring about trophies and all that peace-and-love nonsense.

After all, this competition was called the *Battle* of the Bands, and Troy Bolton knew one thing about battles: the goal was to win.

CHAPTER SIX

After the showdown in the auditorium, Troy really didn't want to approach Ryan for help of any kind at any time. But three rehearsals later, he had to face facts. They needed help. Now.

He caught up with Ryan after study hall. "Hey, can I talk to you for a sec?" Troy asked.

Ryan looked around wildly, searching the corridor for someone, *anyone* else Troy could be talking to, but everybody had vanished into their classrooms.

"Who, me?" he said weakly.

Ryan's mouth twitched as he looked at Troy. The poor guy looks like a scared rabbit, Troy thought. He didn't see how Ryan could possibly help the band, but Gabriella had seemed pretty sure, so . . . "Yeah, you." He jerked his head toward an empty classroom. "In here."

They stood by the blackboard, facing each other warily. "Okay, I know this is weird," Troy said, "but the guys and I . . . well, we need some help with our band."

Ryan shook his head, confused. "You're playing rock 'n' roll," he said. "All I know about are show tunes."

"Yeah, I know. We don't need help with the music. Or"—he added honestly—"not much, anyway. But we definitely need help with . . . well, *looking* like a rock band. You know what I mean?"

"Oh, yeah." Ryan nodded knowingly. "Appearances are half the battle! If not more!"

"Right, so, here's the thing. . . ." Troy hesitated,

59

then plunged ahead. "Would you be willing to coach us a little?"

Ryan's eyes widened in shock. "Coach?" he said, astonished. "You?" He glanced around, wondering if perhaps people were hiding in the supply closet, just waiting for him to take the bait. "Is this a trick?"

"No, I really mean it. I think you could help us. A lot," Troy said. "Look, I know it might seem a little weird, considering how competitive we were during auditions for the musical. But there were no hard feelings in the end, right?"

"Nooo," Ryan said slowly. "Not really." Although, he thought, Sharpay had taken a vow to win the lead in next year's musical, no matter what. And when Sharpay says "no matter what"—as Ryan knew from bitter experience—there was only one thing to do. *Back away slowly . . .*

"And dude, let's face it—you're an awesome dancer!"

Ryan's eyes narrowed with suspicion as he

tried to figure out what was happening here. For some reason, Gabriella's algebra lessons flashed through his mind, and he started imagining an equation that would explain this bizarre moment in his life:

$$\text{(Troy Bolton, basketball star)} + \\ \text{(compliment on Ryan's dancing)} - \\ \text{(any apparent sarcasm)} = X.$$

So that meant that X was . . . ?

Ryan shook his head. No, it was no use. This just did not compute.

"And that dance you and Sharpay did for the musical audition . . . " Troy was going on. "That was great. Lots of rhythm, lots of flash—exactly what my band needs more of."

Hmm, Ryan thought. Troy didn't sound as if he were making fun of Ryan. In fact, he sounded . . . well . . . sincere.

Ryan stood a little taller. "It's true. In fact, I think that routine was a major breakthrough for my work—" Then he felt a sudden wave of panic roll over him. *No! What was he thinking?*

Was he insane? There was no way he could do this!

He whispered in a worried voice, "The only thing is . . . well, my sister—"

Troy held up his hands. "Say no more. I totally get it."

Ryan smiled with relief. Of course, Troy knew all about Sharpay. He would be the first person to understand why Ryan couldn't possibly help Troy's band, no matter how much they undoubtedly needed his talent, vision, and energy. . . .

"We'll be sure to cover your tracks," Troy went on. "So can we start tomorrow afternoon?"

Ryan's smile faded. He didn't remember agreeing to Troy's plan, but apparently he had. He felt a flutter of nerves in his stomach. "Sharpay will be really, really mad—" he began.

"She'll never find out," Troy said confidently. He winked at Ryan. "Trust me."

As Troy was talking to Ryan, Gabriella had slipped into the empty choir room. She walked slowly around the room, remembering the times that she and Troy had rehearsed here for the musical auditions. It had been so much fun, and they had connected so well, and she had felt so free and fearless as she sang with him. . . .

How in the world had she ever let Ms. Darbus talk her into singing a solo?

She slumped down in a chair, her head in her hands.

"Gabriella?"

She looked up to see Kelsi looking at her shyly, a sheaf of music clutched in her arms.

"Are you okay?" Kelsi asked.

Gabriella laughed a little and shrugged. "Oh, yeah, I guess. I'm just having a sudden attack of ultimate stage fright—and I haven't even started practicing my song yet!"

Kelsi smiled and waved away her fears with a jaunty flip of the hand. "Oh, don't worry about that! Ms. Darbus and I picked out a perfect song for you to sing. It's called 'These Boots Are Made for Walkin'.' You're going to love it!"

Gabriella sat up straight. Despite her misgivings, she felt a wave of confidence surge through her at Kelsi's words. "Really? Because I've never sung a solo before and—"

"Nothing to it!" Kelsi sat at the piano and placed her fingers on the keys. "Now, let's get started. . . ."

The next afternoon, Ryan slipped into the auditorium wearing sunglasses, plain black sweatpants, a black sweatshirt, and a black baseball cap pulled down low over his forehead. He was thanking his lucky stars that Sharpay's band was not rehearsing until later that day. In fact, she was, at this very moment, across town in her weekly tap dance class, but she would be back at school in a few hours to rehearse with her group. And she had made it clear that he had to be there as well, to start teaching them their moves.

Ryan thought he had just enough time to work on some fundamentals with Troy's band and maybe get a bite to eat before Sharpay came back.

The most important thing, of course, was to avoid detection. Ryan knew he was taking a risk, but he thought he could pull it off. All he had to do was keep his head down and stay as inconspicuous as possible—

"Hey, Ryan!" Chad yelled from across the auditorium. Ryan jumped. "What's up, man?"

"Shhh!" Ryan hissed. "Keep your voice down!"

Zeke and Jason slammed through the auditorium doors, jostling each other and joking around.

"There he is, the Man in Black!" Zeke yelled. "What's up with the cat-burglar outfit?"

"Yeah, a person might think you were trying to hide or something," Jason teased. "Maybe from a certain ice princess named Sharpay?"

"Shh! Shh!" Ryan kept hissing. They didn't take the hint.

"Man, she's so frosty, we could throw her in the swimming pool and turn it into a hockey rink," Chad said.

The other boys howled with laughter.

"Hey, guys," Troy said as he walked in the door. He looked at Ryan. "The coast is clear, right?"

Ryan nodded. "For now," he said. "But Sharpay is going to be here in two hours, and you guys better be gone. Long gone."

"We're not afraid of your sister, man!" Zeke protested.

"Really?" Ryan was surprised. "*I* am." He gave them a meaningful look. "Believe me, the closer we get to the Battle of the Bands, the more uptight she'll get. And when Sharpay gets uptight—"

Jason shuddered.

"Yeah, we got the point," Zeke said, nodding vigorously.

Troy clapped his hands. "Okay, then! Let's get started."

Fifteen minutes later, Ryan was wondering just what he had gotten himself into.

"No, no, no!" he cried as Chad tried to do a

twist while playing a solo. "You've got to get down low! Keep your balance! Use your quads to twist back up!"

Chad frowned in concentration, tried to do all those things at once, and promptly fell over.

Jason hit a jaunty rim shot on his cymbal to punctuate the moment.

There was a long silence. "Ow," Chad murmured to the floor.

Ryan sighed. "Okay, you can take five. Now, Zeke."

Zeke gulped. "Yes, sir?" He would never have thought he could be cowed by some little dramaclub dweeb, but Ryan was even tougher in rehearsal than Troy was in basketball practice.

"You're standing in one place like you've put down roots," Ryan said. "I know the bass isn't the flashiest instrument, but try to move a little bit. Nod your head, shift from side to side. . . . Go ahead. Try it."

Zeke took a deep breath and started playing a bass beat while nodding his head.

After a few moments, Troy groaned. "Maybe it's better if he just stands there."

"Yeah, when I think about moving, I forget how to play," Zeke said sheepishly.

Ryan glared at them. "Unacceptable!" he snapped. "A professional keeps working and working until he can perform at the peak of his abilities."

"Yeah, but, see, that's the problem," Zeke explained. "I think this *is* the peak of my abilities."

"Today it is your peak," Ryan answered loftily. "But it will not be your peak tomorrow."

"That's real mystical, Ryan. I feel like I'm in a remake of *The Karate Kid*," Zeke muttered.

"No joke," Chad agreed.

Ryan clapped his hands sharply to get their attention. "You two, go to stage left and practice!"

Chad and Zeke looked around, clueless. Ryan sighed heavily and pointed. "Stage left is over there."

They moved away, relieved to have the pressure off for the moment. Ryan turned to Troy. "Now, let's see what you've got. . . ."

After two hours, the rehearsal for Troy's band had ended. Ryan wiped his forehead, exhausted. He had never worked so hard in his life, he thought. He was going to have to spend a serious amount of time watching MTV; he needed *lots* of ideas if he was going to have any hope of making Troy's band look good! Maybe he should rent some DVDs of old rock bands like The Rolling Stones, too. This gig was turning into quite a challenge, but, in a way, he was enjoying being out of his element. And working with basketball players wasn't nearly as frightening as he had feared. . . .

"Alicia! Charlotte! Taylor!" His sister Sharpay's voice knifed through the auditorium. Startled, Ryan ducked behind some scenery that had been left onstage to be repainted. He couldn't let her see him—she was sure to ask all kinds of impossible questions, like *What are you doing up there onstage*? And his mind would go blank and he would start to stutter and she would be able to tell from the expression on his face that he was hiding something!

He heard her continue. "I told you we had to start rehearsal at six o'clock on the dot! Let me give you a showbiz motto: Punctual Equals Professional!"

"I'm so sorry, Sharpay, my mother insisted that I had to finish my homework before I came back to school, just because I happen to be failing geometry!" Alicia bleated as she ran down the aisle to the stage. "It will never happen again, I swear!"

"I would hope not," Sharpay huffed, her arms crossed in displeasure.

Ryan winced. He knew what that crossed-arms posture meant, and it wasn't good. Carefully, he began edging his way through the forest of wooden tree cutouts, heading for the wings of the stage. As he inched along, feeling his way, he kept one wary eye focused on his sister.

She was now confronting Charlotte and Taylor, who were hurrying toward her, out of breath. "And what are your excuses?"

"My brother said he would drop me off, but he took forever to get ready!" Charlotte cried.

Sharpay nodded grandly, accepting the excuse like a queen accepting a petition for mercy from a lowly commoner. "In the future," she promised, "I will pick you up personally."

Charlotte's eyes widened in delighted surprise.

"Taylor?" Sharpay snapped. "Why are *you* late?"

Taylor's mouth was hanging open as she looked back and forth from one girl to the other. Was Sharpay serious? Did she really expect Taylor to grovel for forgiveness, just because she was a few minutes—okay, ten minutes—late for rehearsal?

Sharpay's eyes glittered dangerously.

Apparently, Taylor thought, the answer to that question was yes.

"Well—" she began. Before she could utter another word, there was a crash from the stage. The girls all turned to see a row of wooden trees falling forward and bringing down the curtain with them, all in what seemed like slow motion.

Backstage, Ryan had his eyes squinched shut and his fingers in his ears. Oh no, oh no, oh no, now she'll catch me for sure, he thought.

But Sharpay was simply staring in shock at the mess of splintered scenery that now littered the stage. The stage on which she was about to sing and dance! The stage that was supposed to be clear for their rehearsal! She blinked, hardly able to take in the true extent of this tragedy.

As she stood there, rooted to the spot in horror, Ryan eased his way out of sight and fled for the side door.

A few moments later, he trotted through the main door of the auditorium, a huge, happy smile on his face.

"Hey, girls, are you ready to get busy?" he called out cheerfully. He came to a dramatic halt and stared at the stage, his mouth hanging open, dumbstruck. "Oh, my gosh!" he cried out. "What *happened*?"

As they all started telling him at once, he smiled to himself, relieved. Thank goodness for my excellent thespian training, he thought. It comes in handy at the oddest times. . . .

CHAPTER SEVEN

Gabriella sat in the school library, alone. She had several books spread out in front of her and was staring at her laptop. She sighed. Her midterm paper on the Civil War wasn't due for weeks, but she thought it would be a good idea to get an early start. Usually, sitting at a library table and working would have made her feel happy, productive, and in control.

Instead, she felt lonely, out of sorts, and, well, a little jealous.

This is silly, she told herself. Just because Taylor didn't have time to hang out after school. They'd only planned to grab a soda and talk. . . .

She shook her head at the thought and opened a book at random. She stared at the page with resolve. This was actually a perfect opportunity to get ahead in some of her classes, maybe even have a little less homework to do over the weekend.

She slammed the book shut, scowling. And that was another problem! What happened to the plans that she and Troy had made for this weekend? They had talked about going to the aquarium or taking a long bike ride or just hanging out and listening to music.

Then he had called her last night to say that he couldn't get together with her. "I'm sorry," he had said. "It's the band. It's just taking so much time—"

"Okay, I understand," she had replied, making her voice calm and reasonable. She had seen enough VH-1 specials to know how fans hated the evil girlfriend who makes the band break up. She wasn't going to be one of *them*. "So you're rehearsing all day Saturday? That's great! But what about Sunday? Maybe we could get together then?"

There had been a long, long pause. Gabriella felt her heart sink.

"I'm sorry," Troy had said. He had sounded sorry, too, unless, of course, he was just pretending. . . . No. She would not let herself think that!

"I really want to see you," he went on. "But the band has such a long way to go, and the concert is only a couple of weeks away! I mean, if you could hear the way Jason plays drums! Is it possible to be born with absolutely no sense of rhythm? I mean, *none at all*?"

She had laughed, as she knew he wanted her to, and said all the right things about how important it was that the band perform at least well enough to avoid total humiliation. Then she agreed that they would go out for a celebration dinner when the Battle of the Bands was over.

But she had hung up the phone with tears in her eyes, and she hadn't been able to concentrate on anything—not even something as undemanding as watching a TV reality show—all evening.

She frowned and flipped another page. And then today, Taylor had rushed up to her between classes and said, "Gabriella, I'm so sorry, but I can't meet you today after school!"

"Oh, okay." She had smiled, trying not to look disappointed. "What's up?"

Taylor had rolled her eyes sarcastically. "It's that Sharpay! She called a special rehearsal today. As if rehearsing four times a week isn't enough!"

"Oh. Well, I guess she just wants you guys to do the best you can," Gabriella had said, forcing herself to smile.

Taylor had shrugged. "Or she's psychotically driven to win every competition she enters," she suggested.

Gabriella had smiled at that, a real smile. "To*mayto*, to*mahto*," she said, and Taylor laughed.

So they ended on a good note. But now Taylor was in the choir room, singing, and Troy was in the auditorium, jamming with his buddies, and she was in the library, all alone.

"There you are!"

Gabriella jumped as Ms. Darbus's voice rang out through the empty library. The drama teacher bustled up to her, all business. "What are you doing in this, this—" She looked around at the still, silent room, so different from the energy and excitement of the theater, and shuddered. "—this mausoleum?"

"Um . . . studying?" Gabriella said.

Ms. Darbus's sharp eyes focused on her and narrowed meaningfully. "I think not," she said loftily. "In fact, *I* think you are hiding out."

Gabriella opened her mouth to protest, then closed it. Ms. Darbus was absolutely right. "I guess I just miss my friends," she said weakly.

"This moping isn't like you, Gabriella," the teacher went on. "And speaking of friends . . . I believe I've noticed a couple of people helping you out in the last week, haven't I?"

Hmm. Gabriella frowned slightly as she considered this.

She had only rehearsed with Kelsi three times, but she loved the song and she already had the lyrics down cold. In her quiet way, Kelsi boosted her confidence more and more; each time they worked together, Kelsi gave her tips on singing better, but then finished each rehearsal by giving Gabriella a list of everything she had done well.

And Ryan had stayed an extra ten minutes after each tutoring session to show her a few simple movements she could do as she was singing. The choreography wasn't elaborate, but it was just enough to give her performance, as he said, "a smattering of the three *P*'s—polish, professionalism, and *pizzazz*!"

Maybe, Gabriella thought, she should focus more on all the good stuff she was getting from the Battle of the Bands, instead of thinking about how much her feelings had been hurt. . . .

She nodded with sudden certainty. "You're right, Ms. Darbus."

"Of course I am," the teacher sniffed. "And I happened to see Kelsi sneaking into the choir room five minutes ago. If you hurry, you may be able to fit in one more practice after school today. . . ."

"Got it." Gabriella grinned as she grabbed her books and headed for the door. "And . . . thanks."

Another week of rehearsals went by, which meant it was also a week filled with spats and frayed nerves and exploding tempers.

Ryan rushed into a rehearsal with Troy's band in the afternoon. First, he taught Troy and Chad a basic rock-star stance—neck of the guitar pointed at the sky, legs planted wide, head thrown back—then had them practice it over and over while he worked with Jason on flipping his drumsticks during the song. Zeke had almost mastered the head bob, so Ryan had him move on to a more advanced stage (a slight shuffle back and forth), then went back to Troy and Chad, who were now working on their air jumps but landing incredibly awkwardly. . . .

Before he knew it, the two hours were up, and it was time to dash down the hall to the choir room. As he ran through the auditorium doors, he spotted Sharpay at the end of the hall. She seemed to have caught a glimpse of him—at least, her head had whipped around and her laser stare had practically pinned him to the wall!

He gulped, reversed direction, and fled down the hall toward the gym. He skidded around a corner, darted through an empty classroom and out a back exit, circled the school, and raced through the front doors—where he found Sharpay standing in front of the choir room, looking at her watch and pointedly tapping her foot.

"You're late," she greeted him.

"Sorry," he said, panting. "Had . . . a few . . . errands . . . to run."

"Really." Her tone was glacial. "Was one of those errands in the auditorium, by any chance?"

He shook his head, too panic-stricken to speak.

"Because I could have sworn I saw you coming out of there five minutes ago—"

"Huh." He tried to think of something else to say, but as usual when facing his sister, nothing came to mind.

After a long moment, she shrugged. "Oh, well. At least you're finally here! Listen, you really need to work with the other girls. I've got my routine down cold, of course, but I can't have my backup singers falling all over themselves. . . ."

As the Battle of the Bands competition got closer, Gabriella found that she was seeing even less of Troy and Taylor. For the past week, Troy had only been able to spare a few minutes before school, and she only managed to have lunch with Taylor one time.

And every second she was with them, she had to listen to them talk about the competition. They told her their worries (they would never learn their songs on time, the other bands were probably much better, maybe they should have chosen a better song). They told her their complaints (the band was still arguing about names, the other backup singers couldn't stay on key, everyone wanted to choose a different song but couldn't they see it was way too late?). They told her their secret fears (they would forget the words of the song, they would trip trying to execute a dance step, people would laugh at them).

Gabriella tried to be a good friend and listen to all this with patience and understanding, but by the end of the week, she was ready to snap. And somehow, she had never found the right moment to break in and let them know that she was competing, too. In fact, she had to admit to herself that there was a little part of her that didn't want to tell them, that liked imagining how shocked they would be when she stepped out on the stage by herself. She thought it served them right, in a way, to be kept completely in the dark until the last minute. . . .

But another part of her knew that she was being childish. She just couldn't seem to figure out what to do about it.

She came home from school one day and threw her books on the kitchen table. She opened the refrigerator door and stuck her head inside, searching for a snack that was not healthy in any way.

"Is everything okay, honey?" her mother asked. She was standing at the counter, chopping lettuce for a salad. She gave her daughter a worried look.

"Fine." Gabriella sighed. "Don't we have anything besides fruit to eat?"

"There are carrot sticks," her mother pointed

out. Gabriella sighed even more heavily, and her mother grinned. "And there's a pint of chocolate-chip ice cream in the freezer. It will probably spoil your appetite, but it sounds like you need it."

Gabriella smiled a little as she grabbed the ice cream from the freezer. "Yeah," she muttered.

"Anything I can help you with?"

Gabriella shrugged. "It's just that I never get to see Troy or Taylor anymore, since they got so involved in the Battle of the Bands. They don't even have time to call me at night to talk on the phone for a little while."

Her mother put the lettuce in a bowl and started cutting up tomatoes. "I can understand why you'd feel left out."

"They don't mean to ignore me," Gabriella said loyally. "I'm sure they don't even realize what they're doing."

"Of course not," her mother agreed. "They're both nice people. But they're caught up in something very time-consuming right now. Speaking of which—how is *your* song coming along?"

"Okay," Gabriella said. She paused, then added shyly, "Pretty good, actually."

Her mother raised her eyebrows in mock surprise. "Pretty good? You must be phenomenal if you're willing to say that you're 'pretty good'!"

Gabriella laughed and blushed. "It's a great song. And Ryan even helped me with a few moves. I mean, I'm not dancing all over the place the way Sharpay does, but it's still fun."

"What do Troy and Taylor think about your number?"

There was a long silence. "Um . . ." Gabriella finally said.

Her mother raised her eyebrows again, but this time in real surprise. "Gabriella?"

"Well . . . I haven't exactly told them yet," she admitted.

"Why not? This is something you're all going through together—"

"I know, I know! But the right moment never seems to come along, and anyway, they're only interested in talking about their own songs, and I wasn't sure for the longest time that I would actually go through with it, and—"

"—and maybe you were feeling a little left out?" her mother guessed. "So you decided to shut *them* out and keep it a secret?"

Gabriella looked glumly at her ice cream bowl. When she heard it spelled out like that, it didn't sound so good. "Well, yeah. Maybe."

"Honey, I don't want to tell you what to do," her mother began. "But—"

"—you're going to tell me what to do," Gabriella finished with a tiny smile.

Her mother shrugged ruefully. "I'm going to *suggest* that you let your friends in on your secret. You'll feel better, and I know that they would like to have the chance to support you the way you've been supporting them."

Gabriella nodded. "Yeah . . . but now that I've waited so long, it's going to be kind of awkward bringing it up, you know?"

"True. But not as awkward as having them

find out the night of the competition," her mother pointed out. "And Gabriella—I'm sure that once this is all over with, you guys will be hanging out together all the time and—" her voice took on a teasing note. "—running up the phone bill to astronomical heights, just like you used to."

Gabriella smiled at that. "I guess you're right. Thanks, Mom."

She always felt better after talking to her mother, she thought. Especially when it meant that she also got to eat chocolate-chip ice cream before dinner.

A few days later, Sharpay was walking briskly down the hall, mulling over her latest problem with her girl group and feeling a familiar sense of frustration and irritation. Charlotte just couldn't seem to stay on key, and when Alicia tried to do the hand movements that Ryan had taught them, she looked as if she were signaling a plane to come in for a landing. It wasn't good, not good at all. And Taylor—Sharpay's irritation grew even more intense when she thought about Taylor. She was . . . well, she was perfect. Which wasn't good, either. The angrier Sharpay felt, the faster she walked, until she was double-timing it down the corridor, past the gym, around the corner—

—where she almost ran into Troy and Chad.

"Whoa! Slow down, Sharpay!" Troy said, laughing. "Unless you're trying to take out the competition by mowing us down?"

"Oh, I'm sorry," Sharpay said coolly. "I hadn't noticed that there *was* any competition."

"Ouch!" Chad couldn't help but laugh at her comeback.

"You'll notice when we take the stage for Battle of the Bands," Troy promised. " 'Cause at the end of the night, Mr. Matsui is going to stand on the stage and he's gonna say, 'The winner of the East High School Battle of the Bands is—'"

Too late, he remembered that they still hadn't decided on a band name.

"Yes, I heard you're having a problem naming your little band," she said sweetly. "May I suggest The Mind-Numbing Neanderthals?"

Chad frowned at that. "We have a million names!" he said hotly. "Great names! In fact, that's the only problem we have! Too many excellent ideas for names!"

She flipped her hair back and smiled haughtily. "Well, you better decide on one soon. A good name is one of the keys to impressing the judges."

"Is that right?" Troy said. "So what's your group's name?"

"For your information," she answered frostily, "it's Sharpay and the Sharpettes."

Chad rolled his eyes. "Figures," he muttered. "What was your second choice? Me, Myself, and I?"

Just then, Ryan rushed up to Sharpay. "I just checked with Ms. Dermot about rehearsal space," he said breathlessly. "I got four o'clock, just like you wanted."

Before she could respond, Chad greeted him with a high five. "Ryan, my man!"

"Oh, hey, Chad," Ryan responded, shooting a nervous sidelong glance at his sister.

She was looking back, her eyes narrowed suspiciously.

"Dude, your moves were awesome the other day—" Chad began.

"Um, yeah, thanks . . . er . . . dude," Ryan interrupted quickly. "Oops, gotta run, late for class. Come on, Sharpay!"

He took her arm and headed up the hall. They moved about two feet before she shook herself free and moved in front of him, blocking his way.

"What was that all about?" she demanded. "How do you know that, that . . . *jock*? And why was he complimenting you on your moves?"

"Oh, um." Ryan thought fast. Unfortunately, his fastest thinking was . . . rather slow. "Well, that is, I'm not sure—"

However, Troy had seen the suspicious look

that Sharpay gave Ryan, and he followed them down the hall. He pretended that he had just been casually walking by when he overheard her question. Totally by accident, of course.

"Oh, Ryan was showing us some of the choreography he created for your group during English class yesterday," Troy said. "It's pretty cool."

"Oh." Sharpay looked nonplussed. On the one hand, she liked getting a compliment, even if it was from her main competitor. On the other hand, the compliment was really aimed at Ryan—and what was he *thinking*, letting other people know what they had planned before the actual night of the performance?

"Well, it's even more fabulous when you see us doing it," she said, recovering quickly. She turned to Ryan. "*Which no one will see until the actual night.* Understood?"

He gulped and nodded quickly.

The bell rang. "Good. See you later," she said, and trotted down the hall.

Ryan looked at Troy with relief. "Thanks," he said. "You really saved me."

"No problem." Troy gave him a light punch on the shoulder. "You're kind of . . . well, part of the team now. And teammates always have each other's back, right? Catch you later."

He headed off for class. Ryan looked after him, stunned. *He* . . . was part of the team? He walked down the hall, dazed.

CHAPTER EIGHT

"**Y**ou're doing great, Gabriella," Kelsi said. "Let's do it one more time, from the top."

"All right. But I'm not sure I'm doing that great," Gabriella said. "In fact, I think that the closer we get to the Battle of the Bands, the worse I sound!"

"That's because you're doing a number on yourself in your head," Kelsi explained. "It's one of the perils of performing. You can really psych yourself out if you're not careful."

"Great," Gabriella said glumly. "Now I don't just have to worry about my voice. I have to worry about my mind, too."

"Why don't we try that visualization technique I told you about yesterday?" Kelsi suggested.

"Okay, why not." Gabriella shrugged. "At this point, I'll try anything."

"All right. First, close your eyes and take a deep breath," Kelsi said.

Gabriella did, and Kelsi began to talk in a soothing voice. "You are standing onstage. The stage is dark. You can hear people in the audience talking. . . . Can you visualize that?"

"Uh-huh." Only too well, Gabriella thought. Her stomach was already doing flip-flops, and Kelsi hadn't even gotten to the scary part!

"Good. Now you can hear Principal Matsui walk up to the microphone. The audience hushes. He says—" Kelsi suddenly raised her voice. "'And now, ladies and gentlemen, Gabriella Montez, singing the sixties classic, "These Boots Are Made for Walkin'"'!' And the spotlight hits you! You can feel the heat, and the glare dazzles your eyes! Can you feel that?"

"Oh, yeah," Gabriella muttered. Now her palms were sweaty.

"You feel a little nervous, of course," her friend added, going back to the soothing voice of a New Age meditation tape. "Your heart is beating quickly. Your breath is getting shallow. So you take a deep breath—" She paused while Gabriella obediently took a breath. "—and you remind yourself that you're not really nervous—you're excited! Those butterflies are the feeling of anticipation! You are filled with confidence as you remember all the hours you spent rehearsing! You are filled with strength because you know with absolute certainty that all your hard work is about to pay off! And you are filled with power because you know that you are about to have *the best performance of your life!*"

Gabriella gasped. She *did* feel strong, powerful, and confident! And she *was* excited about singing!

"So you open your eyes and you sing!" Kelsi finished triumphantly.

And Gabriella did.

Four minutes later, she stared at Kelsi in wonder. Kelsi smiled smugly back.

"Wow," Gabriella said. "I really *can* sing!"

"Told you," Kelsi said.

"Hi, hi, hi!" Sharpay said brightly as she entered the choir room a few minutes after Gabriella and Kelsi had left. "Is everyone ready to put on a show?"

Taylor rolled her eyes. It's not a show, she wanted to say. This is just another *practice*. And we've practiced until we're singing this stupid song in our sleep!

She sighed deeply. She used to love "Stop! In the Name of Love," she thought mournfully. Now she didn't think she'd ever be able to listen to it again.

Even Charlotte and Alicia seemed a little weary at this point.

As Ryan rushed in, Sharpay repeated herself. "I said, is everyone ready to put on a show?"

"You *bet* we are, Sharpay!!!" Ryan cried out, adding an extra bit of verve to his voice to make up for being late—again.

The girls just looked at him.

Oops, he thought. That may have been just a *little* bit over the top. . . .

"I mean," he said more calmly, "I'm so excited to see how you guys do today. I thought the choreography was really coming together last night—"

"Yes," Sharpay interrupted. "Coming together, but not quite there. However, with a few concentrated hours of work today, I'm sure we will get to where we need to be."

"Um, Sharpay?" Alicia raised her hand hesitantly, as if asking permission to speak. Taylor barely kept herself from rolling her eyes in disgust.

"Yes, Alicia?" Sharpay inclined her head

98

regally, and Taylor lost her inner battle. She rolled her eyes in disgust.

"The thing is, I've got, like, a major geometry test tomorrow?" Alicia said, as if she were asking a question. "And I really, really, really need to study? Because if I don't make at least a C, I'm going to flunk for the semester and my parents will kill me? So—"

"So," Sharpay interrupted briskly, "I guess you have a decision to make."

Alicia blinked, confused. "I—I do?"

"Yesss," Sharpay hissed. "Do you want to go down in history as the singer who broke up Sharpay and the Sharpettes?"

"Um, Sharpay, what history are we talking about, here?" Taylor asked. It was time, she thought, to try to inject a slight note of reality into this situation.

Sharpay waved a dismissive hand. "The history that will be written when I am famous, of course! Haven't any of you watched those VH-1 specials? Every famous person always starts from humble beginnings with a small group made up of her close friends. Then, one of those friends decides the demands of stardom—even *reflected* stardom—are just too much. She starts whining about too many days on the tour bus, too many bad meals backstage, too many demanding fans—"

Taylor and Charlotte exchanged confused glances. What tour bus? What backstage meals? What demanding fans?

Sharpay, honey, you are in your own little world, Taylor thought. And it sounds like a really scary place to be.

But Alicia was mesmerized as Sharpay went on.

"That friend ends up quitting the band, going back to her dumpy little hometown, and then dying in obscurity—when she could have clung to the star's coattails and enjoyed a life of fame and glamour!" Sharpay finished with some satisfaction. Her eyes slowly swiveled in order to focus on Alicia. "Is that what you want, Alicia?

To die—alone, forgotten, and poor—simply because you were afraid to fail geometry?"

"N-no," Alicia whimpered.

"Good! So let's get started!" Sharpay said briskly. "Ryan, turn on the music! Girls, line up behind me! And one, two, three, *four*—"

As the music blared from the speakers, Sharpay started singing, again giving an all-out performance, stretching her vocal cords to their limits, doing high kicks above her head, and flinging herself around the room in a frenzy of sixties-style dancing.

Taylor, Alicia, and Charlotte sighed but obediently started singing the backup lyrics and moving across the room, doing the steps Ryan had taught them.

Ryan just stood on the sidelines, admiration gleaming in his eyes. The rehearsal had come so close to falling apart! It was the same old story: some people just didn't have the discipline or work ethic or sheer drive to succeed! They always wanted to take shortcuts. But Sharpay would never do that—and she'd never let anyone else do it either! She had pulled this group together in the nick of time, just as they were about to head down that long, slippery slope to the land of mediocrity.

It was times like these, he thought, when he was just so *proud* that Sharpay was his sister!

CHAPTER NINE

"Okay, how about this?" Chad asked. He held up his hands, as if framing a poster with their name on it and solemnly pronounced, "Order of the Wildcats!"

The other boys just shook their heads. "Dude," Jason said, "that makes us sound like some kind of secret society or something!"

Chad took a deep breath. He was a font of creative ideas, an inexhaustible source of imaginative thinking, a veritable master of marketing—but he was getting just a little tired of having every single one of his band names shot down!

He took another breath, even deeper. "Fine," he said evenly. "How about Howlin' Wildcats?"

They silently shook their heads again.

"Wild Howl? The Red Hot Wildcats? Screamin' Wildcats? The Wildcat Crew?" He stopped, frustrated at the litany of no's. "What if it was spelled some different way? Like, um, Wyldkat Crüe?" He spelled it out for them. "And the *u* would have those two little dots over it," he explained helpfully.

They looked at him as if he were insane.

"Okay, then, *you* think of something!" he snapped, just as Troy and Ryan entered the room.

"What's going on?" Troy asked, sensing the tension.

"We still don't have a band name." Zeke shrugged.

"Oh, that," Troy said. As if he didn't have enough to worry about . . . "Well, let's start rehearsing, okay? It won't matter what our name is if we can't even stay in the same key. . . ."

Half an hour later, the band was in the middle of "Twist and Shout" when Troy sensed that they were going off track. He held up his hand and said, "Okay, guys, let's stop right there—"

But the band kept playing.

"C'mon, we have to start again—"

Chad and Zeke grinned at each other as they started doing random riffs. First, Chad would strum his guitar with dramatic swinging arm movements, then Zeke would match him and add a little jump at the end for good measure. They started laughing at their own antics so much that they completely lost track of what song they were supposed to be playing.

As they kept goofing around, Troy started to get really mad. Was he the only one who cared that they were going to look like idiots in front of the whole school when they tried to play?

"Hey, enough fun and games, guys," he tried again. "We need to get serious now—"

But now Jason got into the spirit of things, too, banging his drums as hard as he could and hitting the cymbals every other beat.

Troy yelled, "Stop! Stop! Stop!"

Finally, the band came to a clanging halt, with just the echo of one last rim shot sounding through the auditorium.

"What's up, dude?" Chad asked. "I thought we were actually sounding pretty good there. For a few seconds at a time, at least."

Troy ran his hand through his hair in frustration. "We never end the song at the same time," he pointed out. "Zeke, you keep forgetting what key we're in. Chad, you can't keep making up lyrics whenever you feel like it! And, Jason, you've gotta keep a steady beat. We're all depending on you to keep us in rhythm. C'mon, guys, the competition is in one week! We gotta get it together."

There was a brief silence as everyone stared down at the floor.

"We were just fooling around a little, Troy," Chad said.

"Yeah, this is supposed to be fun, remember?" Jason added.

"I know it's supposed to be fun!" Troy snapped. "But we also want to win, right?"

They all looked down and shuffled their feet. No one said anything.

Troy glared at them. "We do want to win," he repeated slowly. "Right?"

Finally, Chad shrugged. "Yeah, sure, Troy," he said flatly. "We're out to dominate. Go Wildcats."

Troy looked at them, frustrated and confused. Why was this so hard? he wondered. And why did it feel so weird? "Okay, let's all . . . take five," he said. He walked off the stage and out the door. I just need to cool down a little, he thought as he found an empty bench.

He slumped on the bench and stared into the distance. This seemed like such a good idea a month ago. A great chance to hang out with his buddies, have some fun, and then fulfill every secret rock-star fantasy by bringing a crowd of people to their feet, cheering and yelling their appreciation . . .

The only problem, he thought glumly, was that the hanging-out part was feeling more like work, the concept of fun had totally vanished after the first five minutes of rehearsal, and it was becoming quite clear to him that they'd be lucky if the audience applauded politely when they were done.

After a few moments, Troy realized he wasn't alone. Gabriella had sat down next to him.

"Um . . . is everything okay?" she finally asked.

Troy shrugged. "I saw you standing in the back of the auditorium," he said. "What do you think?"

"Well . . . there's still a ways to go," Gabriella admitted. "But—"

"I don't know what's wrong!" Troy burst out. "We all get along great on the basketball court!

Everyone knows what he's supposed to do; we work together like a team! I thought having a band would be the same thing!"

"Except, on the basketball team, you're the captain," she pointed out gently.

He looked at her. "What's that supposed to mean?"

"Well, you're not the captain of the band," she said. "Maybe you need to back off a little."

He shook his head grimly. "The Battle of the Bands is only a week away," he said. "We can't afford to goof off. I've got to keep those guys on track, or we're going to go down in flames."

Before she could respond, Ryan came running up. "I'm sorry I'm late," he said with a gasp. "I just finished Sharpay's rehearsal! Hurry! I've got to get inside before she sees me!"

Troy sighed. "I guess I'd better get back in there," he said reluctantly.

"Can you hang out for a few more minutes?" Gabriella asked, half hoping he would say no.

But he grinned at her and said, "Believe me, I'd rather hang out with you all afternoon then go back to that train wreck of a rehearsal. I'd rather do nothing except hang out with you, as a matter of fact."

She blushed. "Oh, good. Well, I just wanted to tell you something that I guess I should have told you before, but—" She looked away and finished in a rush. "—Ms. Darbus suggested that I sing a solo in the Battle of the Bands and I said yes and she signed me up and I've been rehearsing with Kelsi and I'm sorry I didn't tell you before because I guess we're kind of competing in a way even though I'm sure that I don't have a chance of winning but I was always listening to all your problems with the band plus I was feeling a little hurt because you didn't ask me to sing with you and because you never had time to hang out anymore so I kept it a secret from you and I'm really sorry."

For a long moment, Troy just looked at her, his mouth hanging open. Then he grinned.

"Wow," he said. "You're singing a solo? That's great, I mean, that's really brave. I can't wait to hear you!"

"Really?"

He nodded, suddenly realizing that there had been something else missing from his life for the last month. When was the last time he had been able to sit down and really talk with Gabriella? He couldn't even remember. "And I'm sorry, too, about being so busy all the time," he added. "I guess I got a little too caught up with the band and let it kind of take over my life. I promise, when this whole thing is over, I'll make it up to you. Okay?"

"Okay." Gabriella smiled.

The doors burst open and Ryan ran out, frantic. "Troy! Come on! I only have an hour before I have to meet Sharpay to go over last-minute costume changes!" He made a little "hurry up" motion with his hand, then ran back inside.

Troy gave Gabriella a little shrug. "I gotta go," he said. "Thanks for, you know . . . listening to all my problems. Not just today, either. For the last four weeks."

"Anytime," she smiled, and she meant it.

As Troy entered the auditorium through the side door, he could hear the other guys talking.

"I've just about had it with this band!" Chad complained. "I mean, come on! We're not going on tour or anything! Why do we have to work so hard?"

"Yeah, Troy acts like we're about to be signed by a big record company," Zeke agreed.

"And like he's the guy who's in charge," Jason groused.

Troy stopped, his mouth hanging open. He couldn't believe what he was hearing. These guys were supposed to be his friends! And here they were, dissing him behind his back!

But would they say all these bad things about you if they weren't really upset? A little voice in his head—the part of him that was always way too honest—whispered to him. *Maybe you should hear them out. . . .*

He slipped into the shadows backstage and continued to listen.

"And *nothing* we do is ever good enough!" Zeke went on.

Troy winced. *That* was hard to hear.

But maybe, his brutally honest little voice whispered, *Zeke actually has a point? You have been riding everybody pretty hard.*

Hey, don't be so tough on yourself! Ah, at last! The other little voice, the one that always stood up for him, chimed in. *You were just worried about how the band would sound on the big night. You had their best interests at heart!*

Jason kicked his drum set, making the cymbals jangle. "Hey, I've got a good name for this band, Chad! How about Troy Bolton and the Benchwarmers? 'Cause that's all we are, just a backdrop for Troy to be the star."

Ow. Neither of his voices had anything to say about *that*.

Troy decided it was time to step out of the shadows. As he walked onto the stage, the others fell silent.

"Oh, um, hi, Troy," Chad said sheepishly. "I—we didn't know you were standing there."

Zeke and Jason gave each other embarrassed glances. "Yeah, listen, I didn't really mean—" Jason said.

Troy waved his hand dismissively. "No, that's okay. So, guys, I've been doing some thinking, and I think that an apology is in order—"

"Yes, I totally agree!" Ryan jumped in. "In fact, I'd say that everyone here owes Troy a huge apology!"

Troy tried to stop him. "Actually, Ryan, what I really wanted to say—"

"Don't worry, Troy, I'll handle this," Ryan said. He punched Troy in the arm. "I got your back, buddy." He turned to the rest of the band. "Is Troy being demanding? Yes! Is he forcing you to test your boundaries? Yes! Is he asking you to shoot for perfection? Yes!"

"Um, well, no . . ." Troy tried again.

But now Ryan was on a roll. "He's only being demanding because he wants the very best performance possible! If you could see how Sharpay has been running her rehearsals, you would want to work even harder! They are working day and night! And do you know why? Because you can only succeed through hard work and determination and sacrifice! That's showbiz—and that's rock 'n' roll!"

He finally came to a halt, glaring at the others, hands on hips. For a long moment, there was total silence.

Then Ryan broke the silence by saying, "So. I think *some* people need to apologize!"

Chad, Zeke, and Jason looked down. Chad muttered, "Um, yeah, I guess so—"

"Actually, the only person around here who needs to apologize," Troy interrupted, "is me."

Ryan stared at him in openmouthed shock. The other guys shuffled their feet and muttered things like, "No, that's okay, dude," and "No, worries, man." But Troy had something to say, and he wanted to say it.

"I've been taking this way too seriously, and trying to run the band like—" His mind flashed to Gabriella and he smiled. "—well, like the basketball team. And I'm sorry. I mean, I know it's only rock 'n' roll—"

"But we like it!" Chad shouted. He punched Troy in the shoulder. "That's okay, Troy. We knew you just wanted us to be good. But, man—" He shook his head. "—this band stuff is harder than it looks."

Zeke and Jason nodded.

"Yeah," Zeke said. "It looks so easy on MTV."

"Maybe we just don't have the right stuff," Jason said. "Maybe we should quit."

The other boys nodded and murmured in agreement.

"I. Don't. Believe. What. I'm. Hearing."

They had totally forgotten that Ryan was still there. They turned to see him looking at them in utter shock.

"It's not that big a deal," Zeke said. "So we tried and we couldn't cut it—"

"Failure is not an option!" Ryan barked. "Did you make a basket the first time you tried?"

They all shook their heads.

"Did you dunk a ball the first time you tried?"

They shook their heads again.

Ryan was pacing back and forth. "Did you know how to . . . um . . ." He hesitated. He had come to the end of his minimal basketball knowledge and had to grope for another example. He struggled on. "You know, grab the ball after someone tries to make a basket that doesn't go in—"

"Rebound," Troy said helpfully.

"Right!" Ryan cried. "Did you know how to rebound—"

Chad's eyes brightened and he gave a howl of delight. "That's it! Ryan! Troy! You did it! We've got our name!"

The others looked at him, puzzled.

"Dudes! The band is called Rebound!"

They were all so happy, they started jumping around and high-fiving each other. Even Ryan was in the middle of the boisterous group, with Chad giving him one of his special celebratory high five-low fives.

In the midst of all the ruckus, they didn't notice someone standing at the back of the auditorium, staring at them with anger and shock.

Then the auditorium door slammed shut. Ryan's head whipped around.

"What was that?" he asked nervously.

"Nothing, man," Zeke said. "Hey, Ryan, come over here. Let's work some more on our band choreography. . . ."

CHAPTER TEN

Gabriella had just slowly and laboriously explained the latest algebra problem to Ryan when the door to room 154 slammed open. Sharpay marched in, the light of battle in her eyes.

"How could you?" she yelled at Ryan.

He jumped up and scurried back a few paces. "How could I what?"

"How could you help Troy Bolton with his band?" she yelled, even louder.

Gabriella stood up and tried to intervene. "Sharpay, there's no reason to get upset," she said reasonably. "Yes, Ryan has been doing choreography for both of you, but your bands are so different! It's not as if you guys will be using the same moves—"

"*I don't care!*" Sharpay was screeching now. "You are my brother, and you are supposed to be working for me and nobody but me!"

Ryan stiffened at that. "I'm not your slave! I have talent of my own, you know, and it just so happens that someone else recognized it! And *you* were the one who put together an all-girl group in the first place, so I couldn't even be onstage!"

Sharpay gasped. Ryan had never *dared* to argue with her before! What was going on here? Her universe was spinning out of control! She opened her mouth to yell something else—she wasn't sure quite what, but it was going to be *scathing*—and then looked even more shocked.

No sound was coming out of her mouth.

She tried again, holding her throat.

"Ah, ah, ah," she said.

"Sharpay? Are you all right?" Gabriella was staring at her, concerned.

Ryan just looked scared. "She's lost her voice," he said in a hushed tone. "And just one day before the Battle of the Bands, too!"

Alicia was crying.

Charlotte looked pale with despair.

Ryan was the picture of distress.

Taylor shrugged nonchalantly. "Oh, well," she said. "There goes our chance to go down in history as the founding members of Sharpay and the Sharpettes."

Sharpay gave a little whimper. She was seated, her head in her hands, as the others hovered around her, unsure of what to do. Ryan and Gabriella had helped her to the choir room and explained the situation to Alicia, Charlotte, and Taylor. Now they all stood around, staring at each other.

"We'll have to withdraw from the competition," Alicia said.

Another whimper from Sharpay.

"And my dad was going to bring his golfing partner!" Charlotte cried. "He works for a record label!"

The whimper became a moan.

"Maybe you could try lip-synching?" Ryan suggested feebly.

His sister raised her head long enough to give him a withering look.

"Sorry," he muttered. "I panicked."

Taylor sighed impatiently. "This isn't grand opera, people! There's a very simple solution standing right here in front of us!" She pointed to Gabriella. "This girl is a great singer! I can teach her the song and moves tonight, and she can join the group."

She hesitated, then said to Gabriella, "That is, if you'd be willing to do that. I'm sorry, I know we've all been kind of busy with the Battle of the Bands—well, what I really mean is that *I've* been too busy to spend time with you. And now I'm asking for a really, really big favor. But if you'd consider it . . ."

Gabriella smiled. "Thanks so much, Taylor. It means a lot that you'd ask me. But—" She hesitated, then took the plunge. "The thing is—and I'm really sorry I didn't tell you earlier—but I kind of worked up a little number on my own. A solo."

"Ah . . ." Sharpay's attempt at a scream came out as little more than a gasp. She mouthed the words "a *solo*?" in shock.

"Really!" Taylor beamed at her friend. "That's awesome! What song did you pick?"

"'These Boots Are Made for Walkin','" Gabriella said, relieved at Taylor's reaction. "It's this cool song from the sixties—"

"First sung by Nancy Sinatra, it went to number one in February 1966, a month after its release," Taylor said. "Great choice."

Sharpay gaped at them. They were completely ignoring the major crisis that had befallen *her*!

And her group, of course. She waved her hands in the air to signal that their attention needed to be refocused. On her. Right now.

Ryan saw the wave and loyally jumped in. "What are we going to do about Sharpay's performance?"

"There's a very simple solution," Gabriella pointed out. "Taylor, you know this song backward and forward, and you have a fabulous voice—"

"Yes!" Charlotte squealed. "Taylor, you should take Sharpay's part!"

"That would be perfect!" Alicia agreed.

They clapped their hands with glee. Then Sharpay started whimpering again. They all turned to look at her, and Sharpay saw the truth in their eyes. They had actually forgotten she was there!

A tear rolled slowly down her cheek.

Taylor put her arm around Sharpay's shoulders. "Now, don't cry," she said. "After all, the name of the group is Sharpay and the

Sharpettes, isn't it? We can't go on without you! We just have to figure something else out. . . ."

The auditorium was packed with people the night of the Battle of the Bands. In fact, it was standing room only.

Gabriella stood backstage, peeking through the curtains at the crowd and listening to the excited buzz that filled the room. She gulped. Even after performing the lead role in *Twinkle Towne*, she wasn't totally confident in the spotlight. Actually, she felt as if she was about to faint from stage fright. The only good thing, she thought, is that I'm just singing a solo. Everyone wants to hear the bands rockin' out; nobody will care about my little song. So, no big deal, right?

She closed her eyes and leaned her head against the wall. No. It still felt like a really big deal.

"Hey, Gabriella!"

She heard Troy's whisper behind her and opened her eyes again, smiling.

"Hi, Troy!" She was so happy to see him! All

the memories of performing together in the musical flooded through her mind. Singing onstage wasn't torture, she reminded herself. It was actually really fun! "How are you?"

He nodded. "Okay." He caught the look in her eye and grinned. "Yeah, I'm a little nervous, too. Goes with the territory, right?"

They both laughed softly, showbiz veterans at sixteen.

"Listen, I just came by to say good luck tonight. I mean—" He hastily corrected himself, remembering one of the many lectures on theatrical tradition given by Ms. Darbus. "—break a leg. I'm sure you'll be great."

"Good luck to you, too." She smiled. "I can't wait to see Chad do the twist."

"Yeah, it should be a showstopper," he said dryly, and they both laughed again.

At that moment, Chad's head poked out from the other side of the curtain. "C'mon, Troy," he called. "We gotta get our equipment set up."

"Okay," Troy said. He turned back to

Gabriella. "So . . . tomorrow night? Dinner and a movie? No cancellations allowed?"

"That sounds wonderful."

"Good. See you later." He grinned and dashed off.

Principal Matsui stood in front of the microphone at center stage and cleared his throat. The sound echoed through the room, silencing the energized chatter of the audience.

"Ladies and gentlemen, welcome to East High's first annual Battle of the Bands!" he cried. "I want to thank every student who has worked so hard to bring you all a rockin' good time tonight!" He paused, gratified as the audience's excitement finally translated into the wild applause he had been waiting to hear for so many long, silent months of giving assembly announcements. "First up, we have Troy Bolton, Chad Danforth, Zeke Baylor, and Jason Cross, playing 'Twist and Shout'. Ladies and gentlemen, I present to you . . . Rebound!"

The audience cheered wildly as the curtain rose, revealing the boys standing with their instruments under blue stage lights.

"And one! Two! One, two, three, four!" Troy called out.

They swung into the song, fast and furious. Jason was driving the beat with his wild drumming, Zeke was keeping up with a rapid bass beat, and Troy and Chad matched each other, riff for riff, on the guitar.

Troy started singing the lyrics first, leaping around the stage and striking his very best rockstar poses. Within a few bars, the audience members were dancing and singing along.

Backstage, Ryan watched, his eyes gleaming as all his hard work came to fruition. He was so caught up in the pounding rhythm that he even found himself doing a little dance himself, right next to the wooden tree cutouts.

After the first chorus, Troy backed off and nodded to Chad. Chad nodded back, grinning, and took center stage. He sang the second verse, adding a few spontaneous Wildcat howls, and then did the twist . . . perfectly. The audience went wild, and the boys of Rebound grinned their congratulations.

By the end of the song, Zeke had performed a quick bass solo, and Jason had brought the house down with his special drumstick-twirling technique. The band ended with one loud, triumphant chord, then bowed quickly as the curtain fell.

In the wings, Taylor, Alicia, Charlotte, and Gabriella whispered congratulations as the boys ran off the stage. Sharpay even thawed enough to give Zeke a little wave, which made him grin.

Next, it was Gabriella's turn. She walked onstage, wearing a colorful print minidress and go-go boots. Her hair was done in a sixties-style pageboy with a flip at the ends. She felt totally unlike herself—which was actually a good thing in her opinion. Her knees were shaking and her hands were trembling. It helped to imagine that she was someone else entirely. The spotlight came on, and she blinked. From the corner of her eye, she saw Kelsi give her an encouraging nod as she flipped a switch and the music began playing.

Gabriella started to sing. After the first few notes, she forgot that she was onstage and in the spotlight. She was totally into the song, belting it out with sass and spunk. As she started doing the simple choreography Ryan had designed for her, she could hear some people in the audience yell and whistle.

She dared to sneak a quick peek at the crowd. People were on their feet! They were clapping along! They were smiling! Even Ms. Darbus was doing a little shimmy-shake, right there in the front row. She caught Gabriella's eye and gave her a big thumbs-up.

Gabriella broke out into a huge smile. *Now* she remembered why singing in front of a crowd was so much fun! In fact, she couldn't believe she had ever been scared of it!

When she finished, she bowed and ran off the stage, breathless with excitement.

"You go, girl!" Taylor cried. "That was excellent!"

"Thanks!" Gabriella grinned. She glanced further backstage and saw Troy standing alone. He smiled and gave her a wave of congratulations, but before he could speak, Principal Matsui called out, "And now, ladies and gentlemen, Sharpay and the Sharpettes!"

"Break a leg," Gabriella whispered as Taylor, Sharpay, Alicia, and Charlotte ran onstage. The four girls stood in the spots they had become so accustomed to over the weeks of rehearsal. As the curtain rose, Ryan flipped the switch of the sound system, and the music for "Stop! In the Name of Love" blared from the speakers.

Taylor sang her heart out, her voice ringing through the auditorium with power, confidence, and soul. In the audience, the choir teacher Mrs. Jones smiled with pride.

Gabriella, Alicia, and Charlotte were pitch-perfect as they hummed and doo-wopped away in the background. Sharpay stood next to them, swaying to the music and mouthing the words.

Then, right after the second verse, Taylor stopped singing and moved back to stand with the backup singers. As the music continued its pounding, upbeat tempo, Sharpay stepped forward and began performing the dance that she had planned on doing from the very beginning.

She shimmied. She gyrated. She did high kicks. She whirled across the stage and then whirled back again. . . .

She didn't think it was possible for the audience to scream any louder, but it was. And they were screaming for her!

Sharpay smiled giddily. Maybe she had lost her voice, maybe she couldn't wow them with her singing, but she was right where she always knew she was destined to be—in the spotlight!

When the last group had performed, Principal Matsui told the audience that there would be a fifteen-minute break as the judges' scores were tallied. Gabriella and the members of Rebound and Sharpay and the Sharpettes spent those fifteen minutes backstage, excitedly congratulating each other over and over again for their great performances.

Finally, the principal called all the groups back onstage. He held up an envelope.

"The judges had a very difficult time selecting a winner," he said. "All of the bands performed extraordinarily well. But they finally did choose someone to award the first Battle of the Bands trophy to. And the winner—based not just on talent, not just on hard work, but on incredible dedication in the face of adversity—is Sharpay Evans!"

Sharpay's hands flew to her face in complete surprise—well, almost. It was never really a *complete* surprise when she won, after all.

She rushed forward to take the trophy from Principal Matsui, then grabbed the microphone to address the crowd. She wanted to say what an *honor* this was, how she never *expected* it, and just *how much* all the little people behind the scenes had helped her . . . then she remembered: she couldn't talk.

She frowned slightly, then shrugged and settled for a smile and a heartfelt wave for the audience instead.

As Alicia and Charlotte swarmed forward to hug her, Gabriella murmured to Taylor, "I wonder how long it will be before Sharpay gets her voice back?"

"Not long enough," Taylor said with feeling, and they both laughed.

At that moment, Troy walked past Sharpay. "Congratulations, you really deserved that trophy!" he said. Then he approached Gabriella and Taylor. "Hey, Taylor! Congrats on winning the Battle of the Bands."

"Oh, we didn't win," Taylor said quickly. "Sharpay did."

"I think your singing might have had just a little bit to do with that," Troy said, teasing. "I never knew you had such a great voice!"

"Well . . ." She shrugged modestly.

"Yeah, Taylor, you were awesome!" Chad had now joined the group, still bouncing up and down with excitement. "You, too, Gabriella! And you've got some cool moves!"

"Well, that's all thanks to Ryan. Anyway, it's too bad you guys couldn't have won, too," Gabriella said. "After all your hard work . . . Rebound sounded great!"

"Winning's not the important thing," Troy said. "The best part of forming Rebound was having a chance to hang with my boys."

"You got that right, bro!" Chad declared.

Zeke and Jason ran up. "Hey, you guys, we're all going out for pizza! Do you want to come?"

Everyone nodded eagerly. As they were heading out the side door, Gabriella caught sight of Ryan.

"Hey, Ryan, you've gotta come hang out with us!" she called.

Ryan looked shy, nervous, and hopeful, all at once. "Really?"

"Yeah, of course!" Troy said. "If it weren't for you, none of this would have happened."

"I'd still be standing like a statue when I played," Zeke said.

"I never would have learned to twirl my drumsticks," Jason pointed out.

"And I'd still fall over every time I tried to do the twist," Chad added earnestly.

"Well, okay . . ." He looked at Gabriella. "As long as I don't have to figure out the exact circumference of the pizza . . ."

She grinned. "Consider this a night off from algebra, Ryan! And enjoy it!"

Laughing, they all exited the building into the night.

Something new is on the way!
Look for the next book in the Disney High
School Musical: Stories from East High series. . .

WILDCAT
SPIRIT

By Catherine Hapka

Based on the Disney Channel Original Movie
"High School Musical", written by Peter Barsocchini

"**G**o Wildcats!" Troy Bolton shouted as the basketball left his fingertips. A second later it swished through the basket—nothing but net.

He grinned as his teammates cheered. Troy's best friend, Chad Danforth, raced in and grabbed the ball, then sprang up and dunked it.

"That's what I'm talkin' about!" Chad crowed, doing a little victory dance under the basket.

Meanwhile, a couple of other teammates,

Zeke Baylor and Jason Cross, jogged over to give Troy a high five. "We are so ready for the game next Saturday," Zeke said. "We're going to totally slay Central!"

A whistle blew, echoing through the gym. "That's enough for today, guys." Coach Bolton, who was also Troy's father, surveyed his team proudly. "Have a great weekend, and don't forget that East High's Spirit Week starts on Monday. I expect you guys to lead the way. Nobody has more school spirit than this Wildcats team!" His serious face cracked into a smile as the team cheered. Then he winked. "I also expect to see one of you guys up there reigning as Spirit King at the big dance on Saturday night."

"Gee, I wonder who's going to win that title?" Chad said loudly, putting one finger to his chin and pretending to think hard.

The rest of the guys laughed. Zeke started the chant, and the others picked up on it—"Troy! Troy! *Troy!* TROYTROYTROY!" Chad pumped his fist in the air as he shouted along.

Coach Bolton grinned and strode off toward his office. Troy gave Chad a shove, making him drop the basketball that was tucked under his arm.

"Quit it, bro," Troy said. "If anybody should win that Spirit King title, it's Jason. He's the one who sank that three-pointer that won us the game last week."

"Nice try, Mr. Modesty." Chad scurried after the ball, which was bouncing across the floor.

"Yeah, give it up, Troy," Jason said. "Who could possibly have more school spirit than our superstar team captain? Everyone knows that title is yours—the only question is who's going to be your queen."

Zeke nodded. "Dude, you could show up wearing a hat on Pajamas Day and pajamas on School Colors Day, and you'd still win it in a walk. Nobody can touch you, man!"

"Dad always told me, don't count your baskets until the points are on the board," Troy said, glancing off in the direction in which his father had just gone. "So I'm not counting on anything."

"My man Troy does have a point," Jason said. "Don't forget, the teachers are the ones who make the decision. And who knows how they think? They could decide to give the title to one of their pet science nerds or something."

"No way!" Zeke shuddered, looking horrified. "A science nerd as Spirit King? That's just wrong."

"Yeah," one of the other guys muttered. "But it's possible."

"Whatever." Chad dribbled and shot, sending the basketball bouncing off the rim. "I just remembered, I need to hit the mall this weekend and buy some new pj's. My mom said if I leave the house in any of mine, she'll disown me and go into the Witness Protection Program."

Troy laughed. He'd seen Chad's closet, and he couldn't blame his mom. Every pair of pajamas Chad owned had huge holes in the knees; he was sometimes a little *too* enthusiastic when he played sock basketball in his room. The guy was obsessed. But that was one of the reasons Troy liked him—he was obsessed with basketball, too.

"I still can't believe they want us to wear our pajamas to school," Jason commented as the team wandered toward the locker room.

"Yeah, but think about how comfortable we'll be," one of the other guys said.

"I just hope I can stay awake during physics," said Zeke.

As the guys continued to discuss the pros and cons of Pajamas Day, Troy was thinking about something else. He leaned back against the wall. "Maybe I need to hit the mall, too," he said, mostly to himself. "I want to get something cool to wear next Saturday night."

Chad sidled up to him, dribbling from hand to hand between his legs. "Sounds like someone's already thinking about the Spirit Ball," he said with a smirk. "So when are you going to ask her?"

Troy could feel his cheeks going as red as his Wildcats gym shorts. "I don't know what you're talking about," he mumbled.

But he knew *exactly* what Chad was talking about—Gabriella Montez. Ever since Troy had met Gabriella, she seemed to be all he could think about. She was smart, gorgeous, funny, and sweet. He'd never met a girl like her. Even the thought of going to a school dance with her on his arm, swaying together to the music, made him shiver. All he had to do was figure out the perfect way to ask her. . . .

". . . so he can't ask her," Jason was saying.

"Huh?" Troy blinked, his fantasies dissolving instantly. "What did you just say?"

"Yo, Jason's right," Zeke put in, reaching out and stealing the ball from Chad. "You can't ask her, dude. It's a Sadie Hawkins dance."

"A whosie whatzit?" Chad asked, wrinkling his nose.

"Sadie Hawkins," Zeke explained. He bounced the ball against the wall in time with his words. "That means the girls have to ask the guys, not the other way around."